SANDSTONE
TOWER

SANDSTONE TOWER

Betty Swinford

Copyright © 2005 Betty Swinford

ISBN 1-84550-033-4

Published in 2005
by
Christian Focus Publications
Geanies House, Fearn, Tain
Ross-shire, IV20 1TW
Great Britain.

Cover design by Alister Macinnes
Cover illustration by Colin Sullivan
Bee Hive Illustrations

Printed and bound
by
Nørhaven Paperback A/S, Denmark.

To my son
Stephen
who will be happy to get
another book in English.

Contents

New Home

Jon Rogers stood looking out of the wide picture window. His fists, dug deeply into his pockets, were clenched tightly. Anger was boiling in his heart when Tara came up beside him. He flashed her a sullen look and turned his attention back to the restless, heaving ocean.

"Don't take it out on me, Jon," she chided gently. "Coming to the east coast to live wasn't my idea. But honest, it's not so bad here."

Jon was depressed all the way through to his bones. With a dark sigh he exploded, "I hate it here! Good grief, what are we supposed to do anyway? I can't use my roller blades or my skate board or anything!" he shook his head sorrowfully. "The worst part is that I'll never see my friends again."

It was a rotten deal, that's what. The noise of the screaming gulls and the crashing waves were enough to drive a guy crazy. Jon sighed dismally. He would never get used to it here. Never.

"We can always put up a net and play badminton or volleyball," Tara pointed out, trying to look on the bright side.

Jon snorted and did not reply. He was half a head taller than five-foot-two Tara, even though Tara was a year older. His hair was jet black like his mother's and was determined to hang over the right side of his forehead. Although Jon was tall and well-built, he still resented his lack of good eyesight. His brown eyes were always shadowed by his aviator-style glasses, which were a constant nuisance. However, if he didn't want to see the world as one huge blur, then glasses were necessary until he could get contacts next year. He fumbled around his room like a blind man each morning until he located his glasses.

Tara, on the other hand, had blonde hair that hung nearly to her waist. Her eyes were a dark smoky grey. Jon said she had the sad-looking eyes of a hound dog. Her olive skin came from her Italian mother, and she had a hunch that Jon was envious of her easy tan. Deep dimples dived in and out of her cheeks when she talked or smiled. Her parents had been killed a year before and it was just lately that her dimples had begun to appear once more. The death of her parents was also the reason she had come to live with the Rogers.

That was precisely what proved to be such a source of embarrassment to Jonathon. For Tara wasn't his sister at all; she was his aunt! For pity's sake, people weren't supposed to have babies when they were middle-aged! But Tara had come along all the same, and just one year before Jon was born. Now she called Jon's parents Fred and Maxine. It was sickening, that's what it was, even if Jon's dad was Tara's brother. Boy, just try explaining that to his friends!

"Look out there," Jon growled bitterly. "The waves are too high to swim and we don't even have a surfboard. If those waves get any higher they'll swallow the house."

"Honestly, Jon, the people who built this house planned for high waves," Tara soothed. "Come on, what we both need is to find something to do."

Jon gave her a mock bow. "All right, Wise One, exactly what do you have in mind?"

"Well…" Here pretty face screwed up in a frown. "Why don't we take a look in that old sandstone tower down the beach?"

"Big deal!" Jon snapped. "What is there to see? Boy, Tara, you don't even have a clue."

"But maybe we could go inside and find our way up to the widow's walk. We'd be able to see a long, long way from there."

"Why? To see more water and more sand? No, thanks."

"Jon," Tara said earnestly, her dark eyes gloomy, "do you think all this is easy for me? At least you have your parents. So will you please try to be a little more agreeable?"

Jon clenched his jaw. "I didn't have any problems when I lived in Colorado. There were all sorts of things to do there."

"You didn't even hear me," Tara sighed reproachfully. "You still have your parents. Can't you at least be thankful for that?"

His brown eyes narrowed. "You mean I have my mum," he muttered stubbornly. "Look, Tara, if you want to go to explore some stupid old tower, be my guest. I want to be by myself anyhow."

"Why?" she demanded softly. "So you can go on feeling sorry for yourself?"

Jon didn't answer. He just kept staring at the ocean as though it was partly responsible for bringing him to this awful place.

"Tara! Jonathon!" called a voice from another part of the house. "You can begin putting away your things in a little while."

Tara turned away in defeat and sang out merrily, "Okay, Maxine! I'm going down to the beach to take a look at that old house and I'll be right back."

That old house sat far back from the rolling waves, a great gloomy-looking place with three storeys and a sandstone tower attached to its left side. The tower had been added for the owner's wife, Evangeline Hawkins, a hundred years before. A narrow spiral staircase led to an upper room where she had spent her days painting seascapes. In the tiny room below she had made her afternoon tea and rested before returning to her work. At the very top of the tower was the widow's walk where she would go to watch for the ship that would return her husband from his many sea voyages.

Before leaving the house, Tara poked her head around the corner for one last plea. "Are you sure you don't want to come with me? It'll be a lot better than moping around the house all day, and we might find something exciting."

Jon merely shook his head, never taking his eyes from the rolling surf.

Tara sailed out of the door and felt the cold salty air strike her face. "Goodness," she murmured balefully, "I'm not thrilled about moving here either. I guess I'm just thankful for a place to live. Anyway, getting all angry and bitter doesn't help anything. Maybe it'll be nice living by the ocean."

She kept just beyond the reach of the waves as she walked towards the massive old house. Stopping, she studied the sandstone tower thoughtfully. It loomed, mysterious and lofty beside the house and she wondered where the sea captain had ever discovered the red sandstone.

"How eerie it must look when the fog rolls in," she mused. "I'll have to try and see it if there's fog tonight."

The only other house on the cove was a quarter of a mile farther on. It was perched on a rocky headland beside a big blue lighthouse, but she had no idea yet who lived there.

"The tower has windows in it," she told herself. "But I guess an artist would need lots of light to work by." She shielded her face against stinging particles of sand blown by the wind and stepped to the door of the tower. Scraping away the drifted sand with her foot, she tested the door to see if it was unlocked. It was. She tugged at the door, but it only groaned in protest. Scooping away some more sand, she tried again. Now it opened wide enough to let a blast of mouldy-smelling, age-old air rush out to greet her.

"Well," she beamed triumphantly and stepped inside the tower. It felt chilly and dank, and she did wish Jon had come with her. Not, she quickly assured herself, that she was afraid. But it did feel a little ominous.

At any rate, she was standing on a cement floor with a ragged, stained carpet. The room, of course, was circular. It held a sagging, tattered sofa, a chair with one leg missing, and a small round cast-iron stove that had been used to heat water and to warm the area.

"Not bad," she whispered, shrugging. "Really, not bad at all. So why hasn't someone snatched up the place and restored it?"

Gingerly she crept around the room. Stopping at the bottom of the spiral staircase, she looked upwards. The stairs certainly appeared sturdy enough, but did she really want to go up there all alone?

She was still pondering the mystery of the whole thing when she heard a sound. Chill bumps raced over her body and she stood very still. She was ready to flee if it became necessary. Cocking her head, she listened intently.

After a short time the sound was repeated. Or maybe it was a different noise this time, it was hard to tell. She only knew that her heart was hammering wildly and that her body felt like it was plugged into an electrical outlet.

Persuading herself to move, she backed to the open door a few inches at a time. Reaching it, she spun outside, slammed the door behind her and raced away. She didn't stop running until she reached her home and was safely inside.

"Bogeyman after you?" Jon asked dryly.

"Oh Jon!" she yelped helplessly. "There's someone in that old tower!"

A Face in the Window

Jon's smile was smug and half-hearted. "I should have known. Girls are always afraid of every little thing."

Tara drew back, hurt over Jon's stinging words. "It was dark and spooky in the tower, Jon, and trust me, it wasn't a bogeyman I heard." She hesitated then added, "The tower wasn't locked, either, so anyone could get inside."

Jon's look was pure pity. "The old place has probably been sitting empty for years, so why would anyone bother to lock it? Like I said, girls get all scared over nothing."

It was late afternoon and beginning to get dark. Fog, like wispy grey ghosts, was swirling up over the water, heading for the beach. Jon steeled himself, lifted his chin, trying to look fearless and macho. "I'll not only go inside that tower, I'll spend the whole night there!" After all, Tara's words certainly sounded like a dare! Anyway, no one would miss him. Certainly not his father!

Tara shook her head sadly. "Come on, you know you won't spend the night in that tower."

"Oh no? Just watch me, Miss Scaredy Cat!"

Tara realized he was serious, and now she stopped him with, "Maybe you'd better not do it, Jon. Honest, that old place is creepy."

He ignored her. "Did you say there's a sofa in there?"

"Yes, but it's dirty and ragged. It might even be full of mice or bedbugs." She was sorry for practically daring him to go there and wasn't going to make it easy for him.

Jon's dark eyes narrowed and he muttered, "So? What are a few mice?"

"But, Jon, just look out there. It's getting really foggy. You might not be able to get back home during the night."

His eyes narrowed even more as he growled harshly, "I don't intend to come back here during the night." No way was he going to use the word home, for this place would never be his home! "I'm going to my room to put things away and then as soon as I eat supper, I'm off to that old tower. By then it will be dark and foggy, and you'll see that I'm not one bit afraid."

An hour-and-a-half later, supper eaten and his belongings put away, he waited impatiently for his parents to go to bed.

He didn't have to wait long, for both his parents were weary from unpacking and resettling. Moping around his room, he told himself that it would serve them right if something awful happened to him in that old tower. Then they would be sorry for dragging him across the country and forcing him to live in this hated place.

A gentle rap at his door brought him up sharply and he tiptoed across the room to open it a few inches. Tara stood there in all her wisdom and majesty.

"Well?" she whispered.

"What do you mean, well?"

She smiled drolly. "You're not going through with this, are you?"

"Sure I am!" he hissed. "I just want to make sure Mum and Dad are asleep."

Tara's eyes were troubled. "Oh, they're asleep all right, but seriously, Jonathon, you don't have to prove anything to me. It's a rotten night out there, all wind and fog. I wouldn't blame you one speck if you decide to back out."

Jon grunted. "Oh sure, and let you hang it over my head the rest of my life? No way."

Tara began to look truly worried. "But if something bad should happen to you in that weird place I'd never be able to forgive myself."

Jon grinned wickedly. "All the better to have something to blackmail you with."

"Jon, I'm serious!" Tara stood in the doorway with her hands on her hips, but she could tell that all logic had vanished from Jon now. He was determined to prove to her that he could stay the night alone in the sandstone tower. Or maybe he wanted to prove something to himself.

Biting her lip and fidgeting from one foot to the other, she insisted, "At least take along some food and something to drink. Oh, and you've got to take a good flashlight." She hesitated, looking anxious. "I'm telling you, Jon, it's awful out there. You can't see twenty feet in front of you."

"Oh, like you care!" Jon retorted.

Tara sighed and nodded. "I guess I do care. Look, I know you don't like me living with you, but just remember it wasn't my idea either. I'd give anything for things to be like they were before…you know. But I can't change anything and neither can you, so please, can't we just try and get along?"

Can anything else in my life possibly go wrong? Jon asked himself bitterly.

Tara felt a quick rush of tears and turned to go downstairs to make Jon a sandwich and get him a soft drink to take along on this ridiculous outing.

Entering the room like a black thundercloud, Jon accepted the food Tara had prepared for him, snatched a powerful flashlight, and then got a blanket from the linen closet. He left the house without a word or a backward look.

"Please be careful," Tara whispered after him.

Jon stopped just outside the door, took one look at the fog and dived back inside the house for some candles and some matches. Everyone along this stretch of coastline kept a good supply of candles and kerosene lamps because of the savage storms when they lost electricity.

"Wow, Tara wasn't kidding," he told the foggy darkness and pushed up his glasses. "Maybe I am being stupid to do this." He took a dozen guarded steps forward. The lighthouse's powerful beam might be successful in warning ships of treacherous rocks, but it wasn't doing nearly enough for Jon.

Valiantly, his own light tried to tear in two the ragged curtain of grey that enveloped him, but it was nearly useless. The smell of salt and fish hung heavy on the wet air, but at least the gulls had grown quiet for a while. Breakers were crashing against the shore and Jon supposed the tide was coming in. The low, lonely sound of a foghorn droned into the night, but that only added to the ominous feeling of doom that already filled Jon's heart.

A shudder raced over him and he felt damp and clammy in the drenching fog. Turning around, he tried to decide whether or not to go back to the house. To his amazement, however, it had vanished in the grey mist.

"It feels so eerie," he whispered, afraid to speak aloud. "So...so sinister!"

Horrified at the thought of wandering through the fog all night and having no idea where he was, he thought about praying. Then he shook his head fiercely. That was out! Hadn't he prayed and prayed that his dad would change his mind about moving his family here? Oh yes, and God had politely ignored his prayers.

He stumbled around on the beach for what seemed like hours and suddenly realized that his feet were getting wet. He stopped in his tracks as salt water sloshed over his ankles.

Backtracking quickly, he steeled himself against the black night and the stalking fear. Then the fog parted just enough for him to get his bearings. But to his chagrin, he saw that he was nowhere near the house where he lived, he was standing close to the sandstone tower.

"I don't believe this!" he muttered. "Now I have to spend the night here." Still talking to himself, he groaned, "Serves you right, you idiot!"

Feeling his way around the tower to the heavy oak door, he pulled at it hard. It gave a creak of protest, then began grating along the sand. Opening it just wide enough for him to pass through, he gritted his teeth and went inside. But he was trembling and his heart was a jackhammer.

Standing shivering just inside the door, he shone his light around the room. A gust of wind blew the door shut and he jumped like a startled deer.

Recovering himself, he whispered, "Spiral staircase. I don't know if Tara told me about that or not."

A new kind of dread seized him. What was up there? Oh, wait, he remembered now. Something about the woman who had lived here being an artist and she had an upper room in the tower where she could see out over the ocean. But other than that, Jon knew absolutely nothing about the place.

It was cold and damp. Steadying himself, he went to the small dusty table by the window and lit one of the candles. The tiny flame sent shadows bucking and prancing around the circular room. It also gave Jon a small amount of cheer in his dismal surroundings. Now that the darkness had been driven back a little, he turned off his flashlight to save the batteries.

"Okay, Jonathon," he told himself sternly, "you asked for this." He propped his chin on one hand and thought for a minute. Finally he crossed the room and punched the sofa. "It sure isn't much...springs are practically poking through..." He gazed around some more, wishing there was a fire in the old stove to warm the place. Then, heaving a huge sigh, he murmured, "Guess I might as well try and to sleep, but I'll just leave the candle burning. It won't hurt anything."

He placed half of the blanket over the sofa, gingerly lying down, and pulled the other half over his shivering form. The sofa was smelly and lumpy. Instead of being captured by sleep he was wide awake, miserable and tossing.

It was then he heard a sound from above his head. Startled, he sat up straight, listening intently. His heart had gone wild. He was walking through a minefield of fear!

Were those footsteps he was hearing?

"Get a grip, Jon," he whispered hoarsely. "You're a boy and boys don't panic. Besides, it's probably just your imagination. Tara tried to tell you this place was scary and now you're starting to believe her."

The sound of footsteps stopped as quickly as they had begun and there was a dead silence. Breathing a sigh of relief, he forced himself to lie back down.

It was cold and damp in the tower and again he wished for some wood so he could start a fire in the old stove.

Unable to sleep, he twisted the warm blanket around him and sat up again. Electrified, he grew as rigid as a statue. For there was a face in the window! It was distorted because of the steam on the windowpane from the candle flame, but there was a face! It was a man's face and he was staring at Jon intently!

Woody

It was as though the steamy windowpane and the fog were conspiring together to distort the face. Yet Jon saw one mark of identification that he knew he would never forget. Even if they ran into each other in town three miles away, Jon would know him by the long, jagged scar that ran from the left corner of his mouth to the corner of his left eye. When the cut had been stitched, the eye had been pulled downward, making it a little smaller than the right one.

A shudder rocked Jon's body and he cowed back against the ragged sofa, trying to make himself smaller. Trembling and terrified, he watched as the face withdrew and vanished into the fog.

"He's gone," he whispered to the flickering candle flame. Then he peered warily through the shadows that weaved drunkenly through the ancient tower. A person could be hiding anywhere in those shadows and he would never know it. Someone could be crouching behind the stove, or lying in ambush under the table. They could even be lurking behind the sofa where he sat cringing in his blanket.

He swung his legs over the side of the sofa and reached for his flashlight, trying to swallow his fear. On tiptoe, he crept all around the room. Certainly he was not going to go up those stairs to check things out! He had been stupid to come here, but he wasn't that stupid!

After examining every square foot of the circular room, he whispered gloomily, "Nobody here. But just anyone could barge through that door. There's no lock to keep them out."

He went to look at it anyway. There were two pieces of splintered wood where a plank had once been placed to act as a lock. But the plank was missing and the pieces of wood were useless.

"I'm trapped," he reported, mouthing the words. Crazy as it seemed, it did not feel safe to even speak aloud. "The fog's too thick for me to even think about getting back to the house." He sat down on the three-legged chair, trying to figure it all out. "If I blow out the candle it would be as black as a pirate's flag. I'd really be afraid then. But if I leave the candle burning, then I'm a sitting duck for whoever is out there."

Why, oh why, had he not listened to Tara? Why had he allowed his stubborn pride to do his thinking for him? Exactly who was he trying to impress?

In despair, he looked around for something he could use as a weapon in case the man with the scar decided to invade the tower. All he found was a long, soot-covered stove poker. Wrapping his hands around it frantically, he moved the candle away from the window. That way maybe he would not see the man's face if he returned. And he had something with which to defend himself if he needed to.

"Only now," he whispered dolefully, "I have to stay awake all night so that if the guy does come back, I'll know it."

Something else troubled him too. He was hidden in the shadows facing the door, but now his back was turned to that spiral staircase that led to the room above him. Were all those threatening noises he had heard up there going to terrify him all night or…was someone going to come down those stairs and Jon would not see them?

It was the worst night of his whole life. Every moment seemed like an hour, every hour was like a day. Creaking sounds on the stairs sent shock waves of dread surging through him. The breakers on the beach outside were monsters approaching the tower. Ogres marched through the leaping, flitting shadows cast by the candle flame. He wanted to scream, but that would only draw attention to himself.

His glasses were steamed, so he took them off and wiped them on the tail of his shirt. His eyes drooped with weariness but he dared not go to sleep. The food Tara had fixed for him lay untouched, though he did pop the can of soda and gulped it to moisten his dry mouth. His stomach churned so fiercely that he wondered if even the soda would stay down.

"Tired," he told the reeling shadows. "So tired. If I get out of this mess alive I hope I have the sense to stay away from this old house."

Along towards morning, in spite of his good intentions, his head fell sideways and he dozed. It was the sound of organ music that jerked him sharply awake again.

"Organ music?" he hissed softly.

The sound was low but distinct. And close. Mournful music. It belonged at a funeral.

"Probably mine," Jon whispered in alarm.

The music continued for three or four minutes, then suddenly stopped. The music, however, was immediately replaced by footsteps, which in a way were more ominous that the organ music. The steps seemed to come to the top of the stairs and Jon had visions of someone peering down at him through the shadows. He went into a crouched position, not knowing what to do or which way to turn. It appeared that there was danger outside and danger inside and he was caught between the two.

There's got to be someone in here with me, he told himself in despair. But who? And why?

It seemed an eternity before the grey light of day began to pierce the fog. Heart pounding with hope, Jon went to the door and looked outside. At once the billowing grey wetness blew into the tower room.

He poked his head outside to see if he could locate the house he was now supposed to call home. He saw nothing. Rats! This would never have happened at home in Colorado.

He stepped out into the cold wetness and wished the sun would hurry and burn away the fog. This had certainly been one miserable mistake on his part and he fervently hoped he had learned his lesson.

When finally he could see a few feet in front of him, he closed the tower door and ventured away. Like a fugitive from justice, he crept along he beach, barely able to see the waves rushing towards shore. It was still hard to see, so when he bumped into another figure in the fog, both he and the stranger toppled to the wet sand.

Jon scrambled to his feet, recoiling. His glasses were almost streaming water and he took time to wipe them again. Looking the stranger over, he howled, "You want to watch where you're going?"

For a moment Jon feared he was having a face-to-face encounter with the scar-faced man. It wasn't though. The person was a boy about Jon's own age.

"Hey, I'm – I'm sorry!" Jon sputtered. "I just didn't know anyone else was around."

He took a step back, studying the other boy through the tattered rags of fog. The youth had a stocky build, a thatch of sandy hair and curious grey eyes. He was slightly shorter than Jon and about fifteen pounds heavier.

The other boy got to his feet awkwardly and stood staring at Jon. "Hi. No, it's okay, I should be the one to apologize." He gestured. "I live down on the point by the lighthouse. My dad tends the lighthouse so it's a part of our house." He added the last few words as though they might be an item of interest to Jon. "Who are you anyway?"

Jon thrust out a hand. "I'm Jonathon Rogers. People call me Jon. My dad just bought the house down…well, somewhere down there through the fog."

They solemnly shook hands and the stranger said, "I'm Walter Andrews, but my friends call me Woody." A curious look passed over Woody's deeply tanned face. "So you're the new guy here. Well, I have to tell you, I wouldn't want to live that close to that spooky old house with the tower."

Jon didn't quite know how to answer that. Then warily, "Uh, what do you mean?"

"Haunted," Woody replied firmly. "Everyone in these parts knows the house is haunted. Why, no one even wanted to live in the house you moved into because they refused to live that close to the old mansion. That's why your house was empty for so long."

"You're not serious?"

Woody sniggered. "Serious as a heart attack. I guess the estate agent who sold you the house didn't tell you everything. He'd been trying to unload that place for two years."

Jon frowned, remembering all the mysterious sounds he had heard in the tower the night before. Organ music. Footsteps. Once he had thought he had heard a door close somewhere.

He pushed up his glasses then drove his hands into his pockets. "The estate agent didn't say anything at all."

Woody sighed. "That figures, I guess he wanted to take advantage of newcomers who didn't know anything about the haunted house." Pressing his lips into a fine line, he added, "Too bad."

Jon threw up a hand. "But wait a second: exactly what do you mean by the house being haunted?"

Woody glanced over his shoulder. "Look, I have to get back home, okay? I promised Dad I'd go with him to check his lobster traps as soon as the fog clears. But if you really want to hear the rest of the story about that old house, meet me in front of your house around noon and I'll tell you everything."

He started to move away, but Jon stopped him with, "I know it's none of my business, but just out of curiosity, why were you roaming around in the fog?"

"Oh that," Woody said breezily. "I'm a wood-carver and sometimes after the tide goes out it leaves some really good pieces of driftwood. I always prowl around the beach in the mornings looking at the driftwood. I gather the best pieces, dry them out and carve animals and things." His grey eyes were smiling now. "That's part of the reason I got the nickname Woody." He stopped talking and began to look suspicious. "But hey, I could ask you the same question: why were you out here in the fog?"

Jon frowned and self-consciously placed a finger on the nosepiece of his glasses. "I, um, spent the night in the tower, kind of on a dare. But then I couldn't see how to get back to the house in the fog."

"You've got to be kidding!" Woody hissed.

Jon shrugged and replied sheepishly, "Well, yes I did, and it was the worst night of my life."

Woody shook his head sadly. "You sure wouldn't catch me spending the night there!"

Evangeline Hawkins

For the next few hours Jon brooded over Woody's ominous words. Exactly how much did Woody know about the old house and its mysterious tower? Was he perhaps familiar with its organ playing and its footsteps and moanings?

Jon's parents were still busy unpacking and putting things away. Presently, though, he heard pans rattling in the kitchen and, gloomy and feeling detached from everything, he sat down to eat breakfast. He did wonder how his mum and dad would feel if they knew they had been suckered into buying this house when everyone else had turned it down.

"I called you earlier," his father announced, "and when you didn't answer, I went to your room to wake you. But your bed hadn't been slept in." Mr Rogers' face was faintly troubled. "Would you like to tell me about that?"

Since it was important to Jon to make his father understand how he had messed up his life, he directed his answer to his mother, "Dad's sister," he said in an accusing voice, "dared me to spend the night in that old tower down on the beach."

Tara pulled herself up in straight indignation. "But I also tried to talk him out of it, honest I did, Fred."

Jon winced. He would never get used to Tara calling his father by his first name! "I guess she did," he admitted ruefully, "but by that time I knew I was going to go through with it anyway."

Mr Rogers actually chuckled. Ignoring the fact that his son was still not speaking to him, he confessed, "That sounds like something I would have done when I was a boy." Sobering, he asked, "Did you get some sleep?"

Jon poked at his scrambled eggs. "Mum," he stated emphatically, still not looking at his dad, "it was the worst night of my life."

When his mother answered, there was humour in her tone. "I guess you'll be sleeping in your own bed from now on then?"

"Oh, you can count on that!"

Tara's smoky grey eyes were full of questions. Exactly what was Jon not telling them? She must get him alone somewhere and torture him, if necessary, to make him tell.

John chewed a bite of toast, sipped his milk. Then he asked cautiously, "Mum? Is there such a thing as a haunted house?"

Tara's mouth fell open and she leaned forward eagerly to hear the answer.

Jon's mother looked to her husband for a reply and it was Mr Rogers who answered. But Jon's eyes did not once leave his mother's face.

Laying aside his fork, Mr Rogers dove in. "Jon, there are millions of people who would say yes, that houses can definitely be haunted by departed spirits, especially if tragedies have taken place there. But the Bible states clearly that when people die, they go to either heaven or hell. It says nothing about spirits lingering on the earth." He frowned thoughtfully. "However, it's my personal opinion that evil spirits may occupy such houses. Maybe they're responsible for making noises and such." He sipped his coffee. "Why do you ask?"

Tara's eyes were busy, flashing from one speaker to the next and absorbing every single word.

Still facing his mother, he answered simply, "Woody says that the old house and its tower are haunted and that the reason it has been empty for so long is because the noises have driven people away. He even said that this house was empty for a long time because no one wanted to live this close to the house with the tower."

Jon's mother only smiled, but his father said soothingly, "I wouldn't worry about that. I think the reason this house was empty so long is because most people like to live closer to town. To tell you the truth, I wouldn't mind buying that old place myself. It might make a great inn. The tower would be the perfect place for your mother to write the book she's always wanted to write."

Jon clenched his jaw, wishing his mother would do the talking. To bring that point home once more, he murmured, "Well, I sure wouldn't want to live there, Mum. It's old and smelly and spooky."

Tara had been quiet up until now. Then she spoke up eagerly. "I think it would make a wonderful inn, Fred, and inns are so popular in this part of the country."

Oh sure, Jon thought bitterly, it would just finish wrecking my life, that's all!

He gazed out of the window, where shreds of fog still laced the air. But the sun was shining brightly and it would quickly burn it away. He wanted to get out there and meet Woody so he could hear the story about the old house and its tower.

As if reading his thoughts, his mother said suddenly, "I imagine you two are anxious to get out there and do some exploring, but I'd like you to straighten your rooms first and put away the rest of your things."

"Sure, Maxine," Tara purred, her dimples shooting into position, and again Jon had to grit his teeth at hearing her call his mother by her first name.

The two kids did, however, tidy up their rooms and Tara trailed Jon outdoors. Cornering him at the edge of the creaming waves, she demanded softly, "Is it okay for me to ask what you didn't tell Fred and Maxine?"

Jon faced Tara with a dark look. "Look, they may be Fred and Maxine to you, but they happen to be my mum and dad, so would you please refer to them that way when you're talking to me?"

Tara's mouth dropped open and she took a step back. "Sorry."

Jon tugged a baseball cap from his back pocket, carefully smoothed it and slapped it on his head. "What I didn't tell Mum and Dad," he ground out fiercely, "is that I heard a lot of strange noises last night."

Tara looked at him. "What kind of strange noises?"

Jon's sigh was sluggish. "Organ music and someone walking around. Only no one was there. I saw a face in the window. Someone was watching me."

Tara hopped around on one foot while she shook sand out of her other shoe. "You saw a face in the window?"

Jon nodded dismally, wishing Tara had stayed in the house. "I did. It was a man with a long ugly scar on the left side of his face and – Oh, hi Woody! I didn't see you coming."

Woody perched on a large piece of driftwood and pulled out his whittling knife. With a half smile in Tara's direction, he asked without much interest, "Sister?"

Jon felt trapped and tried to think what to say. "Uh… no. Relative." Saying the word aunt would have been too bitter a word.

Tara threw him a faintly reproachful look and reported quickly, "My name's Tara."

Woody surveyed her coolly then ignored her. Carving the air with his knife, he invited, "Come and sit down, Jon. You still want to hear the story of that old house, don't you? Or should we wait until…?" He glanced at Tara meaningfully.

Tara lifted her chin indignantly. Looking regal and superior, she at once sat down on the other end of the log. "What, I'm not allowed to hear about a house being haunted? Well, I'm here to stay, and for your information, I know all about what happened last night."

Woody stopped whittling to arch his brows and look at Jon questioningly. "Oh?"

Jon's mouth turned down at the corners and he spread his hands helplessly. He felt pretty beat up after losing a night's sleep, but he knew Tara wasn't about to go anywhere so he might as well admit what he had heard the night before. "Well…yes. I did hear things last night. Organ music, for starters."

A twisted grin curved Woody's lips. He ploughed one hand through his thick mane of sandy hair and nodded. "Then I guess you know already that the old place is haunted?"

"And he heard footsteps," Tara injected eagerly.

"Yeah?"

"He heard footsteps, only there was no one there to make them," Tara informed him excitedly.

Jon was gritting his teeth and trying to hold back his anger. "Come on, Tara, will you stop doing the talking for me?"

"Oh boy," Woody muttered.

"What does that mean? Oh Boy," Jon asked wryly.

Woody gestured with his elbow. "My sister is about to join us. Girls!!"

"Well!" Tara teased. "And to think I was just about to tell you what a great wood-carver you are."

Giving her a sheepish grin, he directed his words to his sister. "Might as well come join us, Renee, you will anyway. Meet Jon and Tara Rogers."

"Hi, all," the girl greeted merrily. "I thought there were some kids on the beach our age and, boy, am I ever glad!" Her smile was warm and friendly and Tara liked her instantly.

Her dimpled smile coming into play, Tara announced dryly, "Well, I'm sure glad there's another girl around and I'm not stuck here with two boys."

"You could never do any better," Jon retorted.

Renee was tall and slender, with the same sandy hair as her brother, only her eyes were as blue as the sky and her nose was generously sprinkled with freckles. Tossing her hair back over her shoulder, she planted herself firmly beside Tara and asked, "So what are we talking about?"

With a long-suffering sigh, Woody replied, "We were talking about that old Hawkins' place."

Renee nodded knowingly. "Bet you were just about to tell them the story behind it."

"Right." Turning his attention to Jon and Tara, he began. "See, it's like this. The house was built about a hundred years ago by a sea-captain, Joshua Hawkins. He added the tower for his wife because she was an artist. Of course when houses were built close to the ocean in those days, there was a widow's walk..." Slowly he took up his whittling again, then stopped to ask, "You know what a widow's walk is, don't you?"

Jon was actually paying attention and discovered that he was interested in hearing the story. "Isn't that a place with a railing around it where women went to watch for their husbands' ships coming back from sea voyages?"

Woody nodded absently and carefully sliced off a tiny sliver of wood. "That's right. In the Hawkins' case the widow's walk was put on top of the tower. I guess that's because his wife spent so much time in the upper room painting."

"Especially after the baby died," Renee added sadly.

Woody glanced at his sister reproachfully. "She had a baby there, without a doctor or midwife or anyone, though I imagine the servants helped her deliver it. Anyway, it only lived four months. Captain Hawkins never even got to see it. Evangeline – that was his wife – had to go ahead and bury it without him."

"How awful!" Tara crooned sympathetically.

"It must have been pretty bad," Woody agreed, nodding. He scooped out a tiny chunk of wood with the tip of his knife and continued. "Anyway, the story goes that Evangeline became so depressed that she stopped painting and spent her time pacing around the widow's walk looking for her husband. When he didn't come back she decided that he had been lost at sea."

Pacing, Jon thought, startled. *Footsteps!*

"That would make almost anyone depressed," Tara moaned.

Woody went on doggedly. "Months went by and still Captain Hawkins didn't come home, and Evangeline got to playing funeral music on the old organ up in the tower." His knife stopped completely now. "People in town swore they could hear the mournful music at night when it was still, and sailors nearing the shore said they could hear it sometimes, too. That's how the haunted story got started, because even after she was dead the music kept playing."

Renee picked up the story. "One foggy night Evangeline was so depressed that she threw herself down from the widow's walk and killed herself."

Tara drew in her breath sharply, and even Jon appeared disturbed by the story.

"The really terrible part," Woody reported balefully, "is that two days later the captain came home, but by then the servants had buried his wife. I guess he pretty much fell apart, screaming with rage and grief…"

"He died of a broken heart six months later," Renee sighed.

"But that's awful!" Tara whispered raggedly.

Jon's head was down and his arms were hanging between his knees. Pushing up his glasses, he asked,

"And the haunted part? Is there more?"

Woody's knife stopped moving again as he sank into deep thought. "For years different people tried to live in the house, but no one stayed very long. There were too many weird things going on. They claimed that the captain and Evangeline still lived there. They could hear the baby crying and the captain walking around. They said they could hear the organ playing when no one was there, and one person said they saw Evangeline out on the widow's walk in a long black mourning dress."

Renee nodded, looking very wise. "She always wore black after the baby died. People said they could hear the captain moaning and sobbing for his wife."

They all turned to cast secretive glances at the old house. They sat together in a hushed silence.

Man on the Rocks

"What a sad story!" Tara brooded. "It must have been just awful to live in that big old monstrosity all by herself after her baby died, never knowing when the captain would come back home." She bit her lip. "But the really sad part is that she didn't realize taking her life wasn't the answer."

"Of course," Woody hurried to explain, "there were the servants, but I doubt if they were truly Evangeline's friends. They lived up there on the third floor."

Jon adjusted his position on the warm, damp log. "It's pretty sad all right." His brown eyes showed at least a spark of interest, and for a moment he sat idly chewing a thumbnail. Remembering that Captain Hawkins was rumoured to still be around the house, and tying that in with the face he had seen in the window the night before, he ventured, "About Captain Hawkins, Woody, do you have any idea what he looked like?"

Woody gestured with his knife and gazed out over the restless waves. "Actually, there's a picture of him in town at the museum. He became kind of famous because of the things that happened here and no one ever forgot the story. But let me see…" He laid the knife blade across one cheek. "He was a big man and tall. I remember that. After Evangeline died he always wore black. I guess that sort of matched his dark mood."

Renee's freckled face was intense and she was urging her brother with her eyes. "The scar," she prompted.

Jon leaned forward, squinting from the glare of the sun on his glasses. "Scar?" he echoed with sharp interest.

Woody turned slowly to look at him. "Well, yes, he did have a long jagged scar on the left side of his face. Why?"

Jon hesitated to share with them for fear they would think he was making it up, and Tara was shooting another knowing look his way. He knew that if he didn't tell what he had seen she'd be on him like a bad case of measles. Still he hesitated.

"Oh, I just wondered," he replied slowly and gave Tara a warning look.

Twisting around for a better look at the house in question, he saw it sitting there like some sinister monster from the past. Three storeys high, it had huge bay windows projecting from the front of the second storey. Massive and sturdy, it had survived the savage storms that swept the coast from time to time and probably could be turned into an inn. But with all the eerie stories circulating and with the townspeople undoubtedly adding bits and pieces that weren't even true, who would ever want to stay there?

Woody was watching Jon with keen interest. "What are you thinking?" he challenged.

Jon shrugged and swung his attention back to the little group. "I was thinking that the old place might make a great inn if it weren't for all the wild stories about it. I think as soon as people heard them they'd be afraid to stay there."

Woody carefully nicked a place on the horse's neck and then smoothed it. "Yeah. With its reputation, nobody would want to rent rooms there."

Tara, bright-eyed and dimpled, sat forward eagerly. "Woody, have you or Renee ever actually heard the organ playing or the baby crying?"

Woody's hands fell apart in astonishment. "Are you kidding? Sure we have, especially lately. Some nights when it's real quiet, you can hear that organ playing all the way down to our house. A couple of nights ago when I was prowling around looking for driftwood, I heard the baby screaming. Oh you bet! Listen, I'm no coward, but I try hard to steer clear of that house, especially at night."

Renee decided it was time to change the subject. Brightening, she gushed, "Tara, you just can't imagine how nice it is to have a girl my own age here! It gets pretty boring for me and Woody without other kids around."

Ha! Jon thought bitterly. It's lonesome without my friends around.

"Say, Jon," Woody asked suddenly, "are you a good swimmer?"

Jon shrugged. "Pretty good, I guess. Why?"

"How about you, Tara?"

Tara lifted her chin. "I do okay. I've had swimming lessons."

Well, rah, rah, rah! Jon thought and had to clamp his jaw to keep from saying it aloud.

Instead, he scooted off the log and onto the warm sand. Pulling his knees up to his chin, he asked, "Why did you ask?"

Once more Woody's knife carved the air. "See those big rocks out there? They're about…oh, eighty yards out."

"Sure," Jon responded before Tara had a chance to answer. "I guess you swim out there sometimes?"

Woody nodded. "When the tide is right. You have to be careful, though, because when the tide's coming in, the rocks are almost covered with water and you could never make it back to shore."

"When can we do it?"

Woody grimaced. "We'll see. You have to know exactly which way to swim because there are some mean riptides out there." His mouth turned down and he nodded to himself. "I'll show you sometime," he said, then added piously, "Please don't try it on your own."

Tara's face was full of questions. Her smoky grey eyes fixed upon the crashing breakers that climbed the rocks, she asked curiously, "What's on those rocks?"

It was Renee who admitted ruefully, "Not a lot, just some seaweed and barnacles. Sometimes Woody and I take some fish with us to feed the seals and porpoises." She laughed merrily. "You should see them. They come tearing in like they're coming to a party."

"Really?" Tara beamed. "I would love to see that! But how do you manage to take fish with you?"

"Oh that," Renee said airily. "Woody's so good at making things that he made a tiny raft, and we can put a basket on it to push along with us. Once in a while Dad lets us take the kayak. It's always a lot of fun."

"The porpoises eat right out of our hands," Woody offered, grinning. He saw how quiet Jon had become and turned to him slowly. "Doesn't that sound like fun to you, Jon?"

Jon's sigh was shuddering and resentful. "I'll tell you what's fun. Fun is skateboarding and rollerblading and skiing and tromping through the woods."

"You really don't like it here, do you?" Woody asked in surprise.

"I hate it here!" Jon ground fiercely. "It's not my home and it will never be my home!"

"We have woods," Renee reported gravely. "There

are lots of trees behind the houses. Surely you've seen them."

"It's not the same," Jon told her gloomily.

"You could try our woods," Renee suggested reproachfully. "The trees are thick and there are lots of wild animals in them. Woody and I hike there a lot."

Jon shrugged indifferently and turned his attention back to the great pile of rocks projecting from the water. Squinting, he tried to see and finally pushed up his glasses with a forefinger. Wait a minute! There appeared to be something or someone out there.

"Hey, Woody," he directed, "take a look out there. Don't I see someone on those rocks?"

Woody looked up, knife and the wooden horse motionless. "Weird," he muttered. "Now how did someone get out there without our seeing them?"

"He must be fishing," Renee suggested.

"I didn't hear a motorboat," Jon pointed out, for the moment forgetting how much he hated it there.

Woody shook his head. "He didn't get there in a motorboat."

"A rowboat, maybe?" Tara suggested.

Woody jerked a shoulder. "Maybe. He must have tied it up on the other side of the rocks, because I don't even see a rowboat."

As they continued to watch, a change took place. It was as though the man on the rocks knew he had been detected. Turning slowly he lowered himself out of sight.

Wide-eyed with surprise, Tara hissed, "Did you see that? He ducked down out of sight!"

"I saw it," Woody replied, frowning and puzzled. "He knew we'd seen him so he pulled a disappearing act. But why? Why should it matter that we saw him?"

Jon sucked in a long, slow breath. This place was beginning to be a lot more than he had bargained for. What strange and mysterious events were taking place on this stretch of beach anyway?

The Challenge

It was a stormy time in Jonathon's life. With his mother he was kind and gentle, and he believed that she had not wanted to move to the east coast either. With Tara he tried to be civil, though it troubled him to no end that she had the nerve to be his aunt, and that he had to constantly think up ways to keep that fact a secret.

It was his father he had the problem with. Mr Rogers was a building contractor and had been doing very well in Colorado; so why on earth had he caused this upheaval in his son's life? It wasn't fair. Now his lifelong friends were far away and he was stuck on this crummy beach next to a haunted house!

Alone in his room, feeling depressed, he gave his Bible a sidelong glance. He had not opened it since moving here and it seemed to him that God had taken his father's side in wrecking Jon's life. Still, it was his dad he could not forgive. In all honesty, he wasn't a hundred per cent sure he even wanted to forgive him.

At supper that night, he carefully formed a volcano out of his mashed potatoes, then spooned gravy on the top and watched as it ran down the sides like lava. Not that he was the least bit interested in volcanoes; he simply was not hungry, and he did know that his lack of appetite would make his father feel guilty for making him so miserable and unhappy.

"You're not eating," his mother chided gently.

"I may never eat again," he announced sullenly. "I hate it here!"

Ignoring his remark, Mr Rogers said lightly, "It looks like you and Tara made a couple of new friends today."

"Friends!" Jon snorted with disdain. "Woody and Renee aren't my friends. Maybe they're Tara's, but they're sure not mine."

He watched furtively as his father calmly sipped his coffee. "We live here now, Jon. This is our home, and believe it or not, you will be happy again. Now I want you to act like a mature young man and eat your supper, because moping around will get you nowhere."

Tara sneaked a look at Jon from under her long dark lashes and Jon thought she might be sympathizing with him.

Pushing back his plate, he asked coldly, "May I be excused?"

Mr Roger's voice became stern. "Yes, you may go. Just don't come down to the kitchen for something to eat later."

Jon's eyes were narrow as he jerked away from the table. "Oh, you don't have to worry about that!"

Hoping for some pity from his mother and maybe Tara, he slouched out of the room and headed for the stairs.

It was the telephone call from Woody that roused him from his depression. At ten minutes after nine the sand-haired youth called and Tara brought the cordless phone to his door.

"It's Woody. Do you want to talk to him?"

Jon opened the door just wide enough to take the telephone from her. Then he shut the door and flopped down on his bed. "Hi, Woody."

"Hi. I hope I didn't call too late."

"No, that's okay. How did you get my number?"

Woody's slow drawl sounded on the line. "Easy. I called the operator for new listings. Are you busy?"

"No!" Jon muttered quickly, glad to talk to somebody – anybody. "I'm glad you called."

There was an awkward silence and then Woody murmured, "I know it's got to be tough getting used to a new home."

"It's murder," Jon answered gruffly.

Woody could see at once that Jon would be no help with this conversation. "Well…I was just thinking about something. You spent the night in that tower, right?"

"Uh-huh."

Boy, Jon was not making this easy! "Do you remember when I first met you this morning?" Woody waited until Jon grunted, then asked falteringly, "Did you…I mean, you were so pale it looked like you'd seen a ghost. And I was wondering, did anything else happen while you were there?"

Jon swallowed, moistened his lips and realized with horror that he was becoming hungry, very hungry. "I heard footsteps and the organ music, like I told you before."

"Did you go upstairs in the tower where Evangeline used to paint?" Woody asked breathlessly.

"No. I guess maybe I was…you know."

"Scared," Woody finished for him. "Don't worry, I would have been scared too."

Deciding that perhaps it was all right to share with Woody, Jon signed and confided, "Woody? There was something else."

"Oh?"

"Some guy looked in the window at me. That was what really scared me." Even now, remembering, Jon shuddered and felt gooseflesh rise on his arms like a cold winter wind.

"You saw someone?" Woody echoed in astonishment.

"I sure did, and I hope I never see him again." Jon was quiet for a moment. Then he added reluctantly, "It was a face with a long jagged scar all the way from the left side of his mouth to his eye."

Woody let loose with a few choice slang words. "You saw the captain?" he hissed. "Why didn't you tell me before?"

Jon shrugged. "I was afraid you'd think I was making it up after you described the captain to me." His forehead furrowed in a dark frown, and he stroked into place his flyaway hair. "Please promise not to tell. If people around town know what I told you they'll think I either imagined it or made it up."

"I won't say anything," Woody promised. "But is it okay for me to tell Renee?"

Jon wrinkled his nose. "I don't know. It seems to me that most girls go around blabbing everything they know." That wasn't fair and Jon knew it. Tara was a dedicated Christian and if she said she'd keep a secret, you could count on it.

"If that's the way you want it," Woody agreed. "Only I know my sister and she wouldn't give away a secret if she was being tortured."

Jon thought about that. "It wasn't very nice of me to say that about girls. Tara has known about the face I saw in the window and she's never said a word. Sure, you can tell Renee."

"Your sister's pretty cool."

Jon's frown deepened. "Tara isn't my sister. She's a relative who lives with us because her parents are dead."

Woody whistled softly. "That's got to be pretty tough. And she's so young too."

Jon flinched. Yes, she was young. No doubt about that, his young aunt, who was only a year older than him. Oh brother, he did hope Woody wasn't going to try and squeeze the truth out of him.

"Say," Woody went on, "I just had an idea. Like I told you before, I've heard the organ playing in that old house when no one was there, but I've never been able to work up the courage to thoroughly explore the place. But what if we did it together? Since most of the noises are at night, how about if we spend the night in either the tower or the house? It would be easy for two of us." He hesitated, swallowed hard, and added, "What do you think?"

Jon's stomach was rumbling with hunger and he could have kicked himself for turning his supper down. So much for being stubborn!

He tried to zero in on what Woody was proposing. "It's such a weird old place. I told myself that I would never go in there again, but – " he sighed glumly. "First, let me ask you a question; does the fog roll in every single night?"

"Not every night. But living so close to the ocean, there's a lot of fog. Why?"

"I was thinking that if we did what you said – you know, spent the night there – we'd never be able to get back home if things get out of hand. If, of course, the fog does come in that night."

"It sounds like you're interested," Woody cried eagerly.

Jon pushed up his glasses, then took them off and cleaned them on the tail of his pyjama top. Anything to break the boredom of this place would be welcome. With the two of them, there would be very little danger. Anyway, what could a ghost do to them?

Gulping in a deep breath, he accepted the challenge. "Sure, why not! As long as we're together, nothing can hurt us."

Explorer 340

The boys had agreed to meet on the beach the following morning to talk over plans for staying the night in the old haunted house.

Jon had had a miserable night because of his ravenous hunger and appeared at the breakfast table bright and early to wolf down a plate of ham and waffles.

Mr Rogers grinned wryly. "I see you got your appetite back."

Jon's fork slowed to a crawl. He knew better than to openly combat his father, but the man simply had to understand how he had wrecked Jon's life.

Ignoring his father's remark, he turned his attention to his mother. "I have to get going, I'm supposed to meet Woody." He cast a frown in Tara's direction, hoping she wouldn't insist on tagging along.

"I met Woody early this morning when he was out checking for driftwood," Mr Rogers remarked. "He seems like a nice boy. And, Jon, you'll make even more new friends when school starts."

"I don't want new friends," Jon bristled. "I want my old friends!"

No one bothered to answer, until finally his mother said gently, "Have you asked the Lord to help you overcome your discontent over living here?"

Jon growled something no one could understand. Escaping, he fled from the house, conscious of Tara's watchful eyes following him.

"Over here, Jon!" a voice called, "Hurry, I have a surprise for you."

Jon pushed up his glasses and loped toward the sandy-haired youth. He found him sitting on the other side of a huge pile of driftwood. Gnarled and sun-bleached, it looked like the remains of some prehistoric monster.

Woody was busy whittling, but when Jon came near, he stopped and lifted a hand. "Hi. Give me five."

Jon dutifully slapped Woody's palm. "What's the surprise?"

Woody promptly led Jon toward a kayak waiting on the beach.

"A canoe!" Jon cried, pleased in spite of himself.

"Kayak," Woody corrected proudly. "A 340 Explorer. Inflatable and big enough for two people."

Carefully, he hid his knife and the piece of wood he was whittling at the edge of the driftwood. "Dad said we can use it for a little while if we're careful. I thought, since the tide is out, we could row out to the rocks and fool around. Maybe feed the seals and porpoises."

"That does sound like fun." Sure. It was a whole lot better than moping around the house all day. And it might be interesting.

Woody shoved the lightweight kayak off the sand and into the bluish-green water of the ocean. Hopping aboard with Jon, he murmured, "It feels kind of good to get away without our sisters."

Jon tensed. "Tara is not my sister."

Woody looked up slowly. "Sorry. I keep forgetting." But his expression was one of curiosity and Jon knew it was only a matter of time until he found out what relation Tara was.

"Ever ridden in a kayak?"

Jon shook his head. "No, never."

"Well, put on this life jacket, just sit in the middle seat, and take up that paddle." Woody glanced back at him sharply. "You did say you can swim?"

"I'm not the world's greatest swimmer," Jon confessed, "but I do okay."

"Let's go then. We'll row to the right to keep away from the riptide."

There was a bucket of fish parts sitting between Jon's knees, and already sea gulls were wheeling and screaming at them for their share.

"I guess they know we have treats for them," Jon suggested.

"Oh, you can count on that! Just wait till you see the seals and porpoises come tearing in. They act like spoiled kids."

Woody expertly eased the kayak to the smoother rocks so he wouldn't damage it, then hopped out and tied it to one of the trees that grew there.

Clutching the bucket of fish parts in one hand, Jon followed him. "Boy, this place seems a lot bigger than when I was looking at it from shore. It's almost like a small island."

Woody shrugged. "I guess it is. Only, who would ever want to live here when there's nothing but rocks?" He flung out an arm. "Well, there are the trees, of course, but they look stunted, and twisted like they've been tortured."

It was true. The trees that grew among the rocks were withered and almost black, with hardly a leaf to be seen.

"You would never want to be caught on the rocks when the tide comes in," Woody informed Jon for the second time. "The rocks are just about covered with water. Sometimes it looks like the tide will even catch the house where I live out there on the headland."

Jon was snooping around looking for any evidence left behind by the man they had seen on the rock pile. "Look here," he reported victoriously. "A plastic sandwich bag and a Styrofoam cup that's stained with coffee."

Woody nodded. "So our man ate lunch here." He scratched his head. "But why would anyone want to row out here to eat lunch?"

"I thought we decided he was fishing."

Woody's tanned face scrunched into a frown. "Maybe. But it wouldn't be the greatest place on earth to fish. Look at all the seaweed. A guy fishing here would spend all his time getting his hook un-snagged."

Jon stooped to examine something else. "Oh-oh."

Woody raced to his side. "What?"

Jon lowered his voice to a conspiracy, though there was no need for secrecy. The screeching gulls would have drowned out any sound he would have made. "Look right out there. There's a rowboat headed our way right now."

Woody shielded his eyes from the sun glaring off the water. "I'll bet it's the same guy."

"Hard to tell. But who else would it be?"

Woody snickered. "Aha! Look at him now. He's seen us, so he's pretending to be out there fishing."

Jon's glasses were slipping down his nose from the moisture. He pushed them back into place. "It's strange all right."

The two boys tried to put the stranger out of their minds as they prowled around the rocks searching for other clues. All they found, however, was the shredded end of a rope the man had used to tie up his boat the day before.

"Guess those jagged rocks took care of the rope," Woody nodded.

Jon added ruefully, "I guess you noticed how he tied up on the other side of the rocks so no one on shore would see his boat and know someone was here."

"Except we did know he was here," Woody muttered. "Oh well, he's not coming here now, not as long as we're here. Let's feed these greedy creatures and go on back."

Jon had been so intent in his search that he had hardly heard the barking seals and the squeaking porpoises. Now the sounds brought him to full attention.

"I never saw seals in the wild before," he murmured, more to himself than to Woody.

Woody grinned enthusiastically. "It's pretty neat, all right. I never get tired of them. And those porpoises sound like squeaky toys. But they all want their share of the treats."

"They seem almost tame," Jon whispered in awe.

Woody tossed out a fish and watched as a seal came partway out of the water to catch it, then clapped its fins together, demanding more. They dived and leaped through the water like acrobats, and the porpoises especially looked as if they were happy and smiling.

Woody threw back his head and laughed. "What did I tell you? They're just like spoiled children."

Jon discovered that he was laughing softly as a seagull and a seal had a brief struggle over a small fish. Well, it was kind of a bright spot in an otherwise boring day.

When the fish parts were all gone, Woody rinsed the bucket and set it aside. The sea creatures appeared to know the juicy morsels were gone and they scampered away to search for their own food. Only a few gulls remained, settling down on the rocks and screaming out their indignation because the feast had ended.

"We have to go back," Woody announced reluctantly. "I promised Dad I'd only keep the kayak out for a little while."

"Did you say your dad is a fisherman?" Jon asked without really caring.

Woody nodded. "He sets lobster traps, then sells the lobsters to tourists or to a local restaurant. He also tends the lighthouse there on the point where our house is." Woody hesitated, then added, "If you'd like, we can go out on the boat with him sometime and you can see how the traps work and everything. I mean, I know you don't like it here, but it might be something interesting to do."

"Sure. Okay," Jon agreed without much enthusiasm. "That would be cool."

Woody climbed down off the rocks and untied the kayak. "Oh, and about staying all night in that old haunted house. When do you want to do it?"

Jon shrugged and cried, "Ouch!" When his foot came down on a sharp rock. Positioning himself in the kayak, he took up his paddle. "Whenever you want." Impulsively he blurted out, "Tonight if you want to," and could have bitten off his tongue the moment the words left his lips.

A Creepy Night

Was he out of his mind? It was only the night before last that Jon had spent that miserable night in the sandstone tower, and here he was about to repeat that horror! There must be something wrong with him.

Sadly, however, Woody promptly agreed, for he had never had anyone to share such an adventure with. If Jon backed out now, he was going to look like a yellow-livered coward.

"Let's bring some food along," Woody suggested eagerly before they separated.

Jon was worrying at an unruly strand of hair with the fingers of one hand. "Blankets," he stated with authority. "It gets really cold in that old place at night. Oh, and good flashlights."

"We could gather some wood and make a fire in the stove." Now that he had a companion for this venture, he was really getting into it. Whenever he had suggested such an idea to any of his other friends, they had always found a reason at the last minute why they couldn't do it. He did hope that Jon would not try to wiggle out of it. But that old mansion sure did have the respect of everyone around.

"Um…Tara won't try and come with us, will she?" Woody asked anxiously and bent to pick up his knife and the horse he was whittling.

Jon laughed scornfully. "Are you kidding? She'd be so spooked that if there was any little noise she'd go running and screaming into the fog."

Woody grinned at this picture, then looked at Jon hopefully. "Are you starting to be a little happier here?"

Jon's lips went into a thin line and he shook his head fiercely. "I will never be happy here!" Squinting at the ocean, he repeated the word. "Never."

Woody hesitated. "I don't know if this will mean anything to you, but my mum says that when things are rough it helps to pray about them." When Jon barely nodded, Woody continued doggedly. "What could it hurt? I mean, I don't pray much myself, but maybe it would help you."

Jon was suddenly restless and shifted from foot to foot. "You're a Christian?"

Woody shrugged. "No. Not yet anyway. But my mum is and so is Renee. They think my dad and I will come along pretty soon." He appeared mildly surprised. "Why? Are you a Christian?"

Jon dragged in a shuddering breath. "Actually I am." He could not meet Woody's honest grey eyes. Instead, he fixed his attention upon a tiny eddy of water swirling down into the sand and wished it would sweep him in with it. "It's just…it's been a real bad time for me, moving here and all." He decided not to add that he was bitter and resentful toward his father. If he did that, he might lose the only contact he had here.

"Sure," Woody murmured sympathetically, "I can understand that. But honest, Jon, I'd like to be your friend. If you'll let me."

Guilt shot through Jon like a tidal wave. Woody was acting more like a Christian that he was, and that bothered him a lot. "Thanks, Woody," he said limply.

"Okay, look, I have to go, but what time shall we meet tonight?"

"How about right after supper?" Jon was no dummy, he wasn't about to play the sullen role and skip supper again! "Say, about six-thirty, while it's still light outside." His mouth turned down. "Of course the fog could be rolling in by then."

Woody grinned impishly. "But that will only add to the mystery of the whole thing. Anyway, if there's fog, just watch for my light. I have a really good one that's made to cut through the fog."

With that, they finally went their separate ways. But by the time Jon reached the house his shoulders were slumped and his face was a mask of despair.

A nearby voice said suddenly, "I see you guys managed to get away without me and Renee."

Jon lifted his gaze to see Tara and Renee sitting together on the porch step. "Kayak," he explained shortly. "Only room for two."

Renee bristled teasingly. "You mean Dad let you two go off in his beloved kayak? I'll bet you paddled right out to those rocks to snoop around."

Jon gave in long enough to smile at her. "What are you, a fortune-teller?"

Renee laughed now. "Just smart, that's all. I know how boys' minds operate!"

"Well, we did go out to the rocks, but there wasn't much to see. A Styrofoam cup that had had coffee in it and a plastic sandwich bag." He started to pass on by, when he turned long enough to add, "Oh, we did see a guy in a boat heading our way, and we thought it was the same man. But then he saw us and started fishing."

As he went on inside the house, the two girls had their heads together in animated conversation. Jon decided that the girls were certainly beginning to be close friends, but he did hope that Tara had not told Renee that she was his aunt. He would like to save himself that embarrassment as long as possible.

At six-thirty that evening, Jon and Woody met as planned. A bank of fog was moving steadily towards the shore, blanketing everything it touched. The first few stars would soon be cowering behind the milky grey mist and the mood would dangle like some ghostly thing in a horror movie. Already, the great sweeping beam from the lighthouse was warning ships of treacherous rocks. The foghorn moaned drearily through the oncoming night.

"Do your mum and dad know what we're up to?" Woody asked in a low voice.

Jon made a face. "I didn't exactly tell them. Anyway, I don't much think they care what I do any more."

Woody frowned. He was shocked by Jon's words. "I told my mum and dad what we're doing, but they didn't say much. Mum doesn't believe in ghosts and Dad thinks we're just a couple of kids out for a great adventure. I doubt if he thinks we'll really go through with it anyway."

They walked slowly toward the sinister old house, clutching their blankets and some sandwiches. The fog was stalking them.

Trying to remain calm, Jon asked, "What if the door into the house is locked?"

"I know another way in through the tower," Woody replied in a hushed voice. "There's a small doorway leading from the tower into the house and the lock is broken." He giggled nervously. "I can't believe you actually saw the ghost of Captain Hawkins! I guess that would make a believer out of my mum."

"I guess so," Jon answered doubtfully.

The breeze sweeping in off the water was cool now and the fog was marching toward them steadily. They were at the tower door when Jon suddenly grabbed Woody's arm.

Alarmed, Woody gasped. "What's the matter?"

"A light! I thought for sure I saw a light in the upper part of the tower." Jon pointed. "Through that little window."

Woody cocked his head to look up at the window. "Naw," he scoffed. "Couldn't be. I know there's no one staying there."

"But I'm almost positive I saw something." Jon persisted.

Woody turned the big brass doorknob and stabbed the darkness with his light. "It must have been the light from the lighthouse reflecting from a window pane."

"Maybe," Jon frowned.

"I'll tell you what." Woody stopped long enough to close the great oak door. "We'll go upstairs and check it out just to be sure. Then I'll take you into the house."

The narrow spiral staircase seemed sturdy enough, so they slowly made their way upward.

Woody's swift intake of breath stopped them both in their tracks. The organ was playing, the notes rising and falling mournfully.

It only lasted for a moment, though, and then a heavy stillness settled inside the stone tower. Wanting to hear the sound of his own voice, Woody managed through a dry throat, "Evangeline only played funeral music after her baby died."

"Uh-huh."

The air inside the tower was cold and clammy and neither boy had remembered to bring wood for a fire. Still holding their blankets around them snugly, they took a few more wary steps forward.

"Are you all right?" Woody whispered.

Jon answered with a breathy, "Yes."

They went on up softly and found themselves in a small room with three windows facing front and sides. Off to their left sat the ancient organ, covered with dust and cobwebs, its carpeted pedals that forced air into the bellows ragged from use. Jon shone his light over it and saw at once that while cobwebs hung like lacy grey curtains all over the instrument, some of the keys had no dust at all.

Shivering, he mentioned, "Well, there's no one up here to play the organ."

Woody was grim and suspicious. "But we did hear it, Jon, you know we did."

Jon flung out his arms in a helpless gesture. "You don't have to try and convince me, I heard it the same as you." He flashed his light around once more and stopped when the beam landed on a short flight of very narrow stairs. "Where do those go?"

Woody motioned with his head. "Widow's walk. Come on, let's go…" He broke off and his eyes grew wide with alarm. "Did you hear that?"

Jon nodded shortly. He was ready to bolt, but he couldn't let Woody know that. "It's the same thing I heard when I spent the night here," he whispered.

"Footsteps. Only there was no one to make the footsteps."

Woody, too, looked as if he was ready to shoot down the stairs and dash out into the foggy night. "There's no one here now, either."

Trying not to sound too hopeful, Jon asked solemnly, "What do you want to do?"

Woody was puzzled. "Look, ghosts can't hurt you, can they?" He looked at Jon furtively. "I mean, they can't, can they?"

Jon braced himself. "My mum says –" He sure wasn't going to give his dad any credit for this! " – that dead people don't hang around on the earth after they die."

Woody grimaced. "I know. My mum says the same thing. But…"

Jon thought about telling Woody what his father had said about the possibility of evil spirits infesting places where tragedies had happened but decided against it. No sense bringing even more terror into this tense situation.

Woody clomped down the stairs and stood in the middle of the room with the fingers of one hand tucked inside the waistband of his jeans. "Listen, I don't know about you, but I don't intend to let something that may or may not be real get the best of me."

"I'm with you!" Jon croaked and hoped he sounded confident. Then he played his light across the room, trying to ignore the ominous drone of the foghorn. "Okay, then, let's go inside the house."

Caught in a Trap

Like burglars in the night they tiptoed across the floor to the far wall, their lights picking out the faint outline of a small door. Once it had been locked by a simple wooden device, but it was gone now, so all they had to do was give the door a firm push. It creaked open, sounding like a dozen squealing mice.

Cobwebs shrouded the opening, making it appear that a crew of inspired spiders had been at work. Woody swept them aside impatiently. Ancient smells rose about them, and the floor, though solid, was littered with shredded wallpaper and stuffing from old furniture. For certain, mice had been industriously making nests from any material they could find.

"It sure is cold and damp" Jon whispered raggedly, afraid that if he spoke aloud his voice would crack from the terror of the unknown.

Woody nodded. "These old places always get cold and damp, especially along the beach. This house hasn't been lived in for a long, long time."

The boys entered a large room with a high ceiling, a room with what had once been a beautiful Oriental carpet. Jon guessed that Captain Hawkins had brought it home from one of his many voyages. A dusty cobwebbed chandelier hung in the centre of the room. Crippled pieces of antique furniture still sat about the room, the good pieces having been carried off by looters long ago.

Jon was puffing white steam and gazing cautiously over his shoulder. He had no idea what he was expecting to see. "I thought furniture was always covered with sheets or something when a house was left to itself."

Woody felt numb with fear. "I don't think the captain cared much what happened to the furniture after what he came home to."

"I don't know," Jon muttered, "it looks like he would have cared about something."

"He didn't!" Woody snapped. He was nervous and had no idea why they were even having this conversation. His sigh exploded into the stillness. "Sorry, Jon, I shouldn't have snapped at you. Let's be honest, okay? We're both pretty uptight in this creepy old house."

"It's plenty weird, all right."

Staying as close together as possible, they crept into the great old ballroom. Ancient straight-backed chairs with ragged red velvet seats lay scattered over the floor. A huge grand piano sat at the far end by a large salt-encrusted window, looking utterly desolate and forlorn. The stool was overturned and there were yellowed sheets of music scattered nearby. Such a terrible silence gripped the house that the boys couldn't even hear the mice busily scratching inside the walls.

Prowling through a number of other rooms, they came at last into the massive kitchen. There they discovered a huge square table that still looked solid enough to survive a couple of wars. Cupboards hung open and empty, the picture of abandonment.

Jon went to the window and shone his light through its grime. An instant later he sucked in his breath loudly.

Woody spun around on one heel. "Now what?"

"Look!"

Woody peered closely and there it was, the face of a man in his late forties or mid-fifties staring back at them! A long, jagged scar marked the left side of his face.

Woody turned white and began to tremble. "But, but," he yelped, "that's Captain Hawkins!"

The instant the man had been detected, he slipped from sight, enveloped in the swirling grey mist.

"He's gone!" Woody exclaimed. "But, Jon he was there! I saw him as plain as day." He snatched a look at Jon. "You saw him, I know you did!"

"Oh you bet," Jon whispered, feeling as limp as a rag doll. "The only thing I feel glad about is that he's out there and we're in here."

No sooner had the words left his lips than they again heard the sound of footsteps somewhere above their heads. A door closed solidly, as if whoever had closed it wanted the boys to hear it. Then there were more footsteps and after a few seconds another door closed.

"But I don't get it," Jon said hoarsely. "The man we saw was outdoors."

Woody lowered his voice until it was barely audible. "Maybe," he mumbled dryly, "he's not out there now." His hand went limp and the beam of his light dropped to the filthy, cracked linoleum floor.

Jon tried to hide the shudder that passed over his long, lanky figure. "Ghosts can walk through walls," he announced gloomily.

Now just hold on a minute! He was beginning to talk as if he actually believed in ghosts!

Woody shone his light up from his waist, turning his face into an evil mask. "That's true," he said, nodding.

"Woody, forget I said that, okay? Good grief, I don't believe in ghosts! It's just that there are so many things happening in this old place that can't be explained." Jon pulled in a long, slow breath. "This whole thing is so weird."

Woody looked up at the rough, dark ceiling beams. "I'll tell you what's weird: I think he's in here with us and trying to scare us away."

"Ha!" Jon snorted with disdain. "How can he scare us away when we can't see through all the fog out there to get away?"

Woody jerked his shoulders impatiently. "I guess he thinks we'll panic and take our chances with the fog."

The boys were standing close together in the musty-smelling old kitchen when a large rat scurried between them and vanished behind the huge black and chrome stove.

"Maybe we should have stayed in the tower," Jon whispered dolefully.

Woody's teeth were clenched tightly to keep them from rattling and his eyes were wide and alert. "If you ask me, I think we were stupid to come here at night anyhow. We should have come during the day when the sun's shining."

"Too late," Jon announced dryly and pushed up his glasses. "We could go back to the tower, though. We left our blankets there anyway, and I'm cold."

The air in the ancient house hung around them like a wet curtain, cold and dank. But the boys were encouraged now to hear only a heavy silence.

"I think he's gone," Woody breathed softly.

A board creaked under Jon's foot, sounding for all the world, like a pistol shot in the stillness. Then a mouse on some secret errand raced across the floor and disappeared inside a wall.

"So you have never explored this old place before?" Jon asked quietly. "Even though you live so close to it?"

Woody wrinkled his nose. "Actually, I've only lived

here for two years. I've been in the tower a few times and found the door leading into the house. I've been in a couple of the downstairs rooms, but all the stories circulating about the place – plus the fact that no one was ever willing to explore it with me – I sort of kept my distance." He grimaced. "And remember, I told you how sometimes I've heard the organ playing and sounds like people moaning and crying."

Jon was about to say something when another sound caught his attention. Turning, they stepped to the doorway that led into the big dining room. From there they could see that the front door was standing open. Outlined against the heavy fog, his black waterproof jacket flapping in the wind like a wounded crow stood a ghostly figure.

The boys stood as if turned to stone, gaping and horrified. They were too far from the door leading into the tower to make a rapid escape, and they certainly were not going to pass the bulky figure standing there in the doorway!

Grabbing Jon's rigid arm, Woody hissed, "Come on!"

Without stopping to think about where he was going, Woody led Jon to the wide curving staircase that led to the second floor and took the steps three at a time.

Dimly, they were aware that the front door had closed again, but they had no idea whether the man was in the house or out in the foggy black night.

Gasping and breathless, they reached the second floor of the house. Weak-kneed and open-mouthed, Jon asked in a strangled voice, "That was him, wasn't it?"

Woody sagged against the wall and slid limply to the floor. "It had to be. I couldn't see his face, but who else could it have been?" He pressed his head back against the damp wall and felt beads of cold perspiration trickle down his face and neck. "Yes, it was him all right."

Jon, pale and shaken, sank to the floor as though all the sand had leaked out of him. He was far beyond trying to figure out whether or not he believed in ghosts. He only knew that this old house was sure living up to its reputation for being haunted. The only other thing he knew for certain was that further down the beach there was a large house with a warm, cosy bed that had his name on it.

It was the swift crashing noise that caused both boys to spring to their feet. It sounded all too close and much too ominous, so they cringed against the wall, afraid to move a muscle.

"Wh-where did that come from?" Jon stammered.

Woody jerked a thumb toward the third floor of the house. "What are we going to do?" he whispered. "We don't dare go up or down, and for sure we can't get home." He shuddered violently. "We just can't go anywhere!"

From somewhere above them a door creaked open. Footsteps sounded. Then from faraway they heard the sad music of the organ rising and falling like notes of doom.

It certainly appeared, Jon thought with a sense of dread, that both Evangeline and her captain were still alive and well in this spooky old place.

The Graveyard

Terrified of going to sleep and terrified of staying awake, the boys somehow got through that long, long night by talking in whispers. They made idle suggestions of escape that they both knew were impossible.

"At least the noises have stopped," Jon whispered once.

"Maybe even ghosts have to sleep sometimes," Woody offered ruefully. "But I do wish we had our blankets. It's so cold and damp and my jacket isn't heavy enough."

"I know," Jon soothed, feeling exactly the same way.

"Kind of a weird way to make a new friend." Woody laughed nervously.

"You said it."

Wait a minute. Friend? Jon mused silently. Well, yeah, maybe. Not that anyone can ever take the place of Nathan Hawthorne and Keith Stevens. They will always be my best friends, even if I never see them again. This thought was so bitter it nearly choked him.

The cold and dampness ate their way through the old house like mice eating their way through a sack of grain. Miserable and stiff, they were afraid to even move lest they anger whoever or whatever occupied the house with them.

"Maybe they're mad at us for coming in here," Woody suggested hoarsely.

Jon hunkered down in the murky darkness. He wanted to at least turn on his light but was afraid he would only draw attention to them.

"Can ghosts see in the dark?" Woody demanded in a whisper. "They can, can't they? I mean spirits do have eyes, don't they?"

Jon's sigh was long and hard. "Honest, Woody, I don't know anything about this ghost business. I know there are lots of people who believe in them, though." He sighed once more and scratched behind his ear, then cocked his head and stared away into the darkness. "But, yes, spirits would have eyes and ears and all that. That's one thing I'm really sure about." His shoulders sagged. "That's about the only thing I know."

"Well," Woody drawled, "I know that we saw Captain Hawkins looking at us through the window. And the noises we've heard are real." He hesitated. "Like that organ playing right now!"

Jon pursed his lips, brooding and quiet. After all, what was there for him to say?

Tara was restless. Tossing from one side of her bed to the other, she kept waking up and peering out into the hallway to see if there was a light under Jon's door. She had gone to his room earlier just to talk and had seen that his bed was still made and there was no Jon to be found.

"I just know he and Woody have gone back to that old house," she whispered to the darkness. "And without me and Renee! Don't boys realize that girls like a little adventure too?"

She did feel a wee bit concerned for him, though, and prayed for his safety off and on during the night. Once, her face wrinkled with worry, she prayed, "Lord, I know Jon still loves You. He's just so resentful over having to move here. He hates it that I'm his dad's sister." A wry smile touched her lips. "Will You help him to see that I didn't choose to be born when I was. Help him to like me and accept me. And – and take away his bitterness toward Fred." She hesitated, then went on with a sigh, "Right now, Lord Jesus, I do feel a little worried about him and Woody in that spooky old place, so will You please protect them? I ask this in Jesus' name."

Sleeping and waking by turns, her night, too, at last came to an end. Tumbling from bed, she went to look out of the window.

"Foggy again!" She moaned, "it's no wonder Jon's having such a rough time adjusting to this place."

At breakfast she tried to explain Jon's absence to his parents. "I'm pretty sure he and Woody spent the night in that old house" she grimaced. Then she added brightly, "But this time it wasn't because I dared him. He did it on his own."

Mr Rogers only smiled and shook his head. "It would be nice if he'd keep us informed of his plans. But, again, I have to admit that if I had lived that close to a house that was reported to be haunted when I was a boy, I'd have done the same thing. Jon at least has Woody along with him."

"I don't know," Mrs Rogers worried. "The idea of him being in that place at night doesn't thrill me at all."

Her husband grinned. "That, my dear wife, is because you were never a boy. I'm sure there are some very logical reasons for believing the old place is haunted." He peered at his wife over the rim of his coffee cup. "I still think it would make a money-making project."

"You mean an inn," Tara said with a dimpled smile.

"Well, I would like to see the inside of the place, but the outside appears to be very solid. I think an inn along this stretch of beach might do very well." He looked up, pondering. "Actually, the haunting business might be just the thing to lure guests to stay there."

Tara turned sombre and frowning. "I don't know, Fred, Woody says no one would ever buy this house because it's so close to the other one. Remember?"

"Why, Tara," Mr Rogers chided "surely you don't believe those rumours."

Tara flung her long blonde hair back over her shoulder. "Right now I'm not quite sure what to believe, and that's the truth. I just know I wouldn't want to live there."

Her brother laughed cheerfully. "Well, if I should buy it, I'll make sure we still live in this house. But just think about it: with everyone in the area so afraid of the house, we might be able to purchase it for almost nothing."

The subject was dropped and they finished breakfast in silence. Tara helped her sister-in-law with the dishes. Then she went to tidy up her room. It wasn't her favourite thing, but since her brother had taken her in, she did her best to show her gratitude in small ways.

Those chores accomplished, she dived out into the fog to find Jon. A weak sun was slowly burning away the fog, but still she could not make out the outline of the old house down on the beach. With her flashlight trying valiantly to stab a hole in the fiendish grey shroud, she plodded toward the Hawkins' place.

"He had better be there," she muttered balefully. "I hope he can hear me call him, because I sure don't want to go inside."

It began to rain, just a slow, steady drizzle through the grey curtain. It seemed to Tara suddenly that the fog was increasing. She stopped walking and looked behind her.

"Oh no!" she cried, beginning to know fear. "But I can't see the house!"

Troubled and confused, she turned around and tried to focus her attention on the sandstone tower. Nothing. Just a steadily rolling, swirling bank of fog and it was raining harder now, sending her hair into dark wet strings and beginning to soak through her clothing.

Real fear crowded into her heart now. "This just can't be right! When I left home I thought the fog was lifting, and now…"

Water seeped into her shoes and washed around her ankles and she realized with fresh horror that she was walking right into the ocean.

Tears slid down her face, mingling with the rain. In terror and confusion she darted back the other way, running pell-mell for she knew not where. With wild sobs engulfing her, she became dimly aware of some tall grey spire emerging from the fog. Then two other tall images rose before her blurred vision.

"Trees?" she whispered. "Am I in the woods?"

At least she wasn't in the ocean with its vicious riptides and cruel breakers. Now if she could just stay calm and remain where she was until the fog disappeared she could find her way back home.

Looking closer, she saw now that the first tall image she had seen was, of all things, an angel! A large granite angel with outspread wings, as though it was protecting someone. Straining for a closer look, Tara saw that near the angel was another large grave marker, this one a cross. Between the cross and the angel was a smaller headstone in the shape of a cherub.

"But, but," Tara stuttered, "I'm in some sort of graveyard!"

This news did not cheer her. Who wanted to be trapped in a graveyard on a foggy morning like this? Certainly she did not.

"Well, I'm here whether I like it or not," she brooded, "so I suppose I might as well find out who I'm sharing this cemetery with."

Stooping close, she shone her light on the fat baby cherub and was astonished to see the name Jedediah Hawkins. "Evangeline's baby boy!" she whispered and saw that her breath was white on the chill air. "How sad. But of course she would have buried him close by."

Feeling a little more at ease now that she knew she was among people who were not exactly strangers to her, she shone her light on the cross. Nodding, she murmured, "Captain Hawkins is buried next to the son he never got to see. That means that the angel – the captain must have put it there after he got back home and realized his wife was dead – yes, the angel marks the grave of Evang- -"

Tara was on her knees examining the names when she stopped talking abruptly. A ghostly grey figure rose from behind the angel. Wearing a waterproof, his scar clearly visible through the drifting fog, was the angry face of a man!

Tara gasped and toppled backwards onto the soggy pine needles. Her smoky grey eyes widened in horror and disbelief.

"I'm going to tell you something for your own good," the man said gruffly, "so I want you to listen carefully. Stay away from that old house. Do you understand?" When Tara nodded dumbly, he went on in the same raspy voice. "Tell your brother and the other kid what I've said. Because if they don't stay away, they are going to be very, very sorry."

Though Tara was cowering and terrified of the misty grey figure, another part of her wanted to giggle. If he thought Jon was her brother, then ghosts must not be very smart.

Game of Cat and Mouse

Tara started to get to her feet but stumbled backwards over a protruding tree root and landed once more on the soggy pine needles. When she lifted anguished eyes, the shadowy figure had vanished. She was alone and terrified.

Wet, sobbing and cold, she looked around wildly, trying to decide her next move. Finally she cupped her hands around her mouth and screamed frantically, "Jon - a – thon! Jon, please, oh please. Help me!"

But the boys were still crouched on the second floor of the house and heard nothing. They, too, were still terrified of the big man with the scar and were afraid he might be in the house with them. They crowded together until morning, cold and shivering.

A heavy grey light at last penetrated the gloom and they rose stiffly to their feet, listening intently for any sound. The organ music had stopped some time ago and an eerie stillness had invaded the old house.

Slithering warily down the stairs, they paused in the deep gloom of the entryway and saw that the big oak door was not securely closed.

"It had to have been that strange man making all those noises last night," Jon reported balefully, not at all sure that this was true.

Woody nodded solemnly and flung back a strand of sandy hair. "I think you're right. I can't imagine ghosts making all that racket."

Jon blew out his breath, thinking hard but still unable to put it all together. He had now seen the face of the mysterious man twice and it certainly seemed to be made of flesh and blood. Still, the description of Captain Hawkins matched it perfectly. He tried to make some kind of sense from it all, but he came up empty. Maybe, he decided, his mother and father were wrong about ghosts, and the spirits of dead people really did hang around places where tragedies had happened.

Woody walked to the heavy front door and gave it a hard tug. Nothing happened. "Well," he exclaimed drolly, "all I can say is that the ghost must have a lot more strength than I have." He jerked a thumb. "Come on, we'll have to go back through the tower."

Creeping through the small doorway they snatched up their blankets and draped them around their shivering bodies. The fog was still weaving its mysteries and its secrets around the tower, turning the outside world into a place as ghostly as the interior.

"Jo – on!"

They heard the desperate cry for help at the same time and looked at one another sharply.

"Did you hear that?" Woody hissed.

Jon's nose was damp and his glasses were slipping. Pushing them up impatiently, he announced, "That was Tara, I'm positive of it, and she sounded frantic. But where in the world is she?"

Woody motioned to his right. "At back of the house, I think." He wiped one of the small windowpanes with his jacket sleeve and tried to see outside. "The fog's lifting a little. We'd better see if we can find her."

Jon sighed with disgust. Why would she go out there in that fog? Why didn't she use her head and stay inside the house where it was safe?

They rushed out into the rain and closed the tower door behind them. At once the smell of salt and fish and sea assailed them. The foghorn was still wearily moaning, warning ships that there were rocks ahead. Breakers along the shore were high and threatening.

"Tara?" Jon called.

A faraway voice answered bleakly, "Jon! Oh thank goodness! Jon, I'm in some kind of a graveyard." Her voice quivered dangerously. "But I'm not alone so please be careful. I think that old sea-captain is in here with me."

At the moment Tara had no idea whether she really believed that. With events rolling so fast it was hard to know exactly what to believe.

"That old guy sure gets around," Woody remarked dryly.

"I guess," Jon admitted grudgingly, "that anyone would be scared half to death if they met up with that man in a graveyard." He glanced at Woody's shadowy figure. "But why would there be a graveyard here?"

"Well, because," Woody was starting to feel more like himself now that they were away from the house and brushed away Jon's question lightly. "See, it's a small family plot. The Hawkins are buried there."

Jon nodded shortly, then yelled, "Tara! Talk to us so we can find you."

"Over here!" she cried limply.

The boys stumbled upon her huddled in terror beside the tall white angel with her face buried in her hands. She was a pitiful-looking figure, with her hair plastered wetly to her head and shaking uncontrollably.

Seeing their approach, she sobbed hysterically. "Oh Jon, thank God you found me! I prayed and prayed you'd hear me. I thought the fog was lifting when I left home to find you, and then it got heavier and I didn't know where I was." She was rambling now but could not stop herself. "Then I found this graveyard and that man with the scar was looking at me and…" She finally stopped long enough to take a breath, but she was crying so hard that Jon couldn't tell the tears on her face from the rain.

Woody poked Jon. "I think your cousin needs you."

Jon bit back an answer. Let Woody believe whatever he wanted about Jon's relationship to Tara. He did, however, feel a swift tenderness for this girl who had helped to further disrupt his life.

Kneeling beside Tara, he took one of her icy hands in his. "It's all right, we're here now and you're not alone. Don't worry, anyone would have been scared stiff to wander into a graveyard in this pea soup. Good grief, this is Frankenstein stuff!"

Tara unexpectedly buried her face against his shoulder. "But the face, Jonathon! It wasn't just anyone's face, it was his, Captain Hawkins!"

"Did he say anything?" Woody asked curiously.

Jon helped the terrified girl to her feet. Keeping the blanket around Tara, he gestured with his free hand. "Let's go inside the tower where it's a little warmer. We can't see how to get back to the house yet anyway."

Tara did not question Jon's wisdom but followed the boys obediently back to the red sandstone tower. Once inside, Jon lowered her to the ragged sofa and wrapped the blanket more snugly around her.

"Do you feel like talking?"

Tara nodded slowly and reached up to part the wet hair from about her face so she could see. "Well, he – the man I saw, the captain –" She threw up her hands in despair. "I know there aren't supposed to be such things as ghosts, but who else could it have been?"

The fellows waited, a little impatient for her to tell them what she knew. Then Jon smiled at her and perched beside her on the smelly old sofa.

Taking a deep breath Tara went on doggedly. "He – he looked at me over one of the headstones and warned us to stay away from this old house. He said if we didn't we were going to be very, very sorry."

"He's a ghost!" Woody snorted. "What does he think he can do to us?" At the sound of footsteps his gaze drifted up the spiral staircase. Dryly he added, "Except scare us to death, of course."

"He is in here!" Jon hissed, his brown eyes troubled. "And I'll bet he's been in here with us all night."

Crowding together like pigeons after breadcrumbs, the three terrified kids waited in dread silence to see what would happen next. Their eyes were all fixed on the narrow staircase now, and next they expected to hear the organ playing.

"Oh dear Jesus" Tara whispered, "please, please take care of us."

Jon absently nodded his agreement and thought how weak his prayer life had become since moving here.

As they continued to watch the stairs, a figure swished past their vision and was gone in an instant. Dark and menacing, the youths knew it was time to get out, fog or no fog.

"Let's go!" Woody prodded.

They were out of the door in a flash. Only Jon took time to close the door, hoping that this action would keep whoever was in the tower from coming after them.

"Did, did you see that person dressed in black?" Woody sputtered. "That was Evangeline. Had to be. She always dressed in black after her baby died. And she's the one who played the organ." He wiped imaginary sweat from his forehead. "Can you believe it? Those people still live there! No wonder no one would ever stay in that house after the Hawkins died."

They trudged along silently, aware that there were now only rags of fog left. Gulls wheeled and dived, screaming, as they searched for fish. Sand pipers industriously marched up and down like toy soldiers, gathering juicy morsels from the sand.

"I can see our house now," Tara ventured.

"I have to go home," Woody reported, stuffing his hands into his pockets. "Maybe we can meet later today?"

Jon nodded. "Sure. But before you go, take a look at the rocks."

Woody shielded his eyes from the morning sun and tuned to see that had grabbed Jon's attention. It had stopped raining minutes before, leaving the rocks dark and glistening. But there he was, the mystery figure who took such delight in that big clump of rocks.

Woody nodded grimly. "He always makes sure he can't be seen from that old house. Unless I miss my guess, that's what he's out there watching, anyhow."

The Beach Party

Only a few wisps of fog were left and a bright sun was warming the earth. Woody had gone off towards home, but Jon and Tara watched with curiosity the man out on the rocks who seemed to be fishing. All these strange, unfolding events lifted even Jon's gloomy spirits a little. They had not, however, taken away the bitterness he felt for his father in moving his family to this stretch of beach and tearing up his life.

Suddenly Tara turned to him. "Do you know where my brother's binoculars are?"

Jon stirred, arched his back and sighed. "I have no idea where my dad's binoculars are."

"Oh come off it, Jonathon!" Tara blurted out. "What do you want me to do, call my brother Dad just to make you happy? Well, he's not my dad, he's my brother, and I can't help that! I don't think it was right for you to tell Woody I'm your cousin."

"I didn't tell him that!" Jon shot back indignantly.

"You didn't correct him when he said it, either, and it's the same thing."

Jon blew out a low, slow breath. "Look, if you think for one minute that I'm proud of the fact that you're my – my aunt, you can think again." He spat out the word aunt as though it left a bad taste in his mouth. Then, mellowing a little, he asked, "Why did you ask about Dad's binoculars?"

"Because," she announced eagerly, "I'm pretty sure the man out there is watching that old house through binoculars. So if we had my brother's binoc- - Oh-oh! He saw us and now he's ducked down out of sight."

Jon put aside their spat of a moment before. "I wonder if it was him in the house making all those weird noises."

Tara's mouth turned down and she shook her head. "Not possible. He was on the rocks as soon as we came outdoors, so he couldn't possible have got out there that fast."

"The whole thing is such a puzzle," Jon admitted ruefully.

"I know." Tara turned her attention elsewhere, the mystery for the moment forgotten. "I have an idea." When Jon looked at her expectantly, she hurried on. "We should know by six o'clock if there's going to be fog tonight, right?"

"I suppose so," Jon agreed dully, tumbling back into his depression. "Why?"

Tara was standing with her head high and her dimples in place, looking wise and knowing. "Well… why don't we have a beach party? You know, the four of us? Woody, Renee, you and me."

"I know who the four of us are," Jon replied dryly. He did not feel the slightest interest in some beach party, but it would be something to do. "What do you have in mind?"

Tara stopped walking and crossed her arms over her chest, her chin in one hand. "We could make a fire on the beach and roast hot dogs. I'm positive Maxine has some buns and some marshmallows in the house, and there are always some soft drinks in the refrigerator. What do you say? It'll be fun."

Jon had to admit that the idea held some appeal. And it meant he would not have to sit across the table tonight from his father and be eaten up alive with that awful resentment boiling inside him.

"Let's turn around and go see what Woody and Renee think of the idea," he suggested.

Leaving the blanket on some driftwood, they walked back down the beach. Carefully they skirted the old house, for even in daylight it appeared sinister and threatening.

But Tara stopped suddenly and deliberately looked at the great, sprawling mansion with its peeling paint, its great bay windows and the pitted sandstone tower. "I know," she said, waving a hand through the air nonchalantly, "we'll have our party right in front of the house just to prove to those ghosts we're not afraid. Anyway, the house sits far enough back that if anything really bad happened we'd still be safe."

Jon wrinkled his nose, which caused his glasses to slip. He pushed them up without thinking. "Sure," he said calmly. "We could do that." After all he was a guy, and guys must never let girls know that their hearts skipped a beat at the very thought of that old house.

After a moment Tara changed the subject. "And Jon? Please don't hate me because I'm your aunt, or my brother for moving us here. Things in life just happen."

Jon turned his head and talked to the ocean. "I don't hate my dad. I just can't forgive him for wrecking my life."

"You want to know something?" she asked gently. "I always used to admire you because you were such a strong Christian…"

"You're not a psychiatrist, so don't play that game with me," Jon retorted sharply. "You haven't got a clue what I'm going through."

After that, tight-lipped and silent, he tromped on through the sand to Woody's house. The spark of interest he had felt in a beach party was dead.

Both Woody and Renee, however, were enthusiastic about the idea, and Renee announced immediately, "That sounds like a great idea, and I'll tell you what: I'll go to the kitchen right now and bake a chocolate cake to bring along." She stuck her thumbs under her armpits teasingly and boasted, "I make a wonderful chocolate cake if I do say so myself, and it doesn't come out of a box either!"

Catching the moment of gaiety, Jon dropped to one knee and quipped, "Marry me and you'll make me the happiest man on earth!"

They all laughed and Jon was again lifted from his gloom and despair. After that, Renee went straight into the house to bake her cake and Tara went to watch. The boys roamed the beach searching for driftwood for their fire tonight. There was supposed to be a full moon, and if the fog stayed away it would be the perfect night for their party.

They met on the beach at dusk and made a fire to roast their hot dogs. Gulls closed in almost at once, screaming and hoping for handouts. Woody found some slender, damp pieces of wood with which to spear the hot dogs and marshmallows. The girls busied themselves by spreading out their food on a large blanket. Even Jon relaxed and was shocked to find that he was actually enjoying himself. Boy, his emotions sure were a yo-yo right now!

"This was a great idea," Woody praised cheerfully. "I don't know whose idea it was, but it was a good one."

"I think it was Jon's aunt's idea," Renee reported innocently, then clapped a hand over her mouth. Her blue eyes were shocked and guilty. "I'm – I'm sorry!"

Jon ducked his head, staring at the crackling flames and wishing the sand would open up and swallow him.

Woody cocked his head, surprised at Jon's embarrassment. "Oh," he murmured softly, "Tara's your aunt?"

Jon stared at his hot dog, which was slowly burning to a crisp in the fire. His ears pounded. His heart was a tomb filled with the dry bones of shame and anger. Still, he had known that the truth was bound to come out sometime.

Tara had shared this information with Renee as a secret, and now Renee tried to cover her mistake. "After Tara's parents were killed she came to live with her brother. Naturally," Renee ended primly. She looked at Tara. "That's right, isn't it?" When Tara barely nodded, Renee hurried on. "I think it's kind of neat, because now Jon has a sister too."

Woody saw Jon's misery and murmured easily, "I'll bet you're right, sis, Tara would be more like a sister."

That was it? No crude jokes? No one was going to make fun of the situation? Jon had done all that worrying for nothing.

"Sure." Tara managed to pick it up now, her dimples deep and merry. "After all, I'm only a year older than Jonathon, so we're a lot more like brother and sister."

Jon could have bowed down and kissed her feet. So it wasn't a big deal at all!

They had just put mustard on their hot dogs and were lifting the tabs on their soft drinks when they wondered if they were about to have company, for there was a boat out in the cove.

If fog was going to roll in, it was still far away. A full moon rode in the sky. Behind them, the old house stood shrouded in mystery. Still, with the stars hanging warm and close and the surf rolling in gently, it was an almost perfect night.

All that began to change as the boat, its motor

sounding over the waves, moved toward them. Almost at once the atmosphere of peace and safety changed, and the four kids watched as the boat scraped shore and three older boys leaped out.

Strutting toward them arrogantly, one of the boys mocked, "You're having a party and I wasn't invited? I'm hurt."

"Billy," Woody warned gruffly, "this is our party, so please just go away and leave us alone."

Another boy spoke up now, a bully with a husky build, broad shoulders, a red crew cut and eyes like drill bits. "Aw, now we're really hurt." Edging around the little group, he drawled, "Well, looky here, hot dogs and everything. Now I just know you brought enough for three hungry guys."

Jon and Woody exchanged looks and Jon saw the alarm in Woody's grey eyes. Evidently Woody knew that these kids were bad news, so Jon decided to keep an eye on Woody and see what he was going to do.

"Come on, fellows." Woody's voice was low and urgent and, Jon thought, held a trace of fear. But at least he wasn't showing any fear. "Why don't you just get in your boat and leave, okay? We're not looking for any trouble."

Billy smirked. "Sure, sure. We will. But we want to eat first, see? I'm sure you wouldn't turn us away when we're so hungry." Turning to his friends, he cried, "Hey, guys, take a look at that! Chocolate cake. My favourite. And pretty girls. I'd say this is our lucky night, wouldn't you?"

Loud and coarse, the other two boys hooted their agreement.

Bending low, Billy got down in Woody's face, and Woody realized there was liquor on his breath. "I'll tell you what we're going to do. Me and my buddies are going to take the girls out for a nice moonlight ride, and if you will solemnly promise to save us that chocolate cake, we'll bring them back safely."

Terror was etched upon the faces of both girls. Tara's dimples weren't showing now. Her face was gaunt and pale and she was stricken at Billy's harsh words. She glanced at Renee and knew that she, too, was white, her freckles standing out in dark patches. She cowered back, too horrified to try and run away.

As for Jon, he was feeling intense indignation. "You," he stated with great authority, "are not taking my…Tara…anywhere."

He might as well have said 'sic em' to a dog, for his words only spurred the three boys onward. Laughing with glee, they moved in close and reached down to take the girls by force.

Both Jon and Woody leaped to their feet, fighting fiercely to defeat the older, stronger boys. They were tossed aside like old shirts and landed in the gritty sand. The beach blanket landed in the fire during the fighting and went in flames. Onions, mustard and all the other food ended upside down on the beach. The chocolate cake flew into the air and landed in a soft mush in the sand. Jon's glasses were wrenched from his face and lost in the flickering shadows.

The girls fought like wildcats, but pitted against the boys' superior strength, their efforts were useless. Still clawing and resisting, they were slowly dragged to the waiting boat.

It was the sound that brought them all to a swift standstill. It was the sad, mournful music from the ancient organ floating dismally into the night. Even Billy and his friends stopped short and gazed wonderingly at the sandstone tower.

"Hear that? Hissed one of the boys.

"Let's get out of here," said another.

"Then let's get the girls in the boat and – " Billy sucked in his breath noisily and his hold on Tara lessened. She fell to the ground like a bag of flour and scrambled over to Jon for protection. Renee, too, seeing a slim chance of escape, ran to her brother and clung to him for dear life.

"L-look at that," whispered one of the boys ominously.

The moon was directly behind the tower, and outlined against it clearly was a figure dressed in black staring down at them from the widow's walk.

Billy swore fiercely. "Evangeline Hawkins! Then it's true, it's all true!" He shoved at the boat and swore again. "Come on, let's get out of this place!"

Seconds later the motor roared to life and the boat scooted far out into the cove, leaving behind it a wake of foaming, surging water. Now the only thing left was the black-clad form up there on the widow's walk.

Going it Alone

Woody gasped out loud, "Can you beat that, girls? Old Evangeline Hawkins just saved your skin."

"Yes, but look," Renee squealed, her face still masked with horror at what had so nearly happened, "she's disappearing now, like – like she's melting down into the tower."

"Stairs," Woody reported dryly. "She's going down the stairs."

Jon was frantically combing through the sand with his fingers in an effort to locate his glasses. "Nobody move, okay? And will you please tell me what's going on? Billy knocked my glasses off and I can't see a thing."

"A woman," Tara whispered. "A woman in a long black dress came out on the widow's walk and scared those awful boys away. But…I still don't see how it could have been Evangeline."

Jon's groping fingers found his glasses at last. He blew away the sand, steamed them with his breath and wiped them on the tail of his blue knit shirt. Since they weren't broken, he planted them firmly on his face again. Looking up at the tower, he moaned, "I sure wish I could have seen her."

"That's all there was to see," Renee told him, her face still pale behind the spray of freckles. "I know ghosts aren't supposed to be real, but who else but Evangeline could it have been in that long black dress?"

Jon was still staring up at the widow's walk. "I did hear the organ playing, but I couldn't see anything. I still don't get it, because if it was Evangeline…"

Woody cut in excitedly. "Look, I know what your mum and dad and my mum says about ghosts, but take my word for it, that was Evangeline Hawkins up there. She came outside just after she played the organ." He made a circle of his mouth and blew out his breath. "And, boy, her timing couldn't have been better!"

Jon cast a helpless look at Tara, but she looked just as puzzled as he felt. "I did see a black figure up there," she announced solemnly. "Just when things looked so bleak for me and Renee." Spreading her hands lamely she added, "It was like she came out on the widow's walk to protect us."

"Well," Jon pointed out ruefully, "they sure did leave in a hurry."

Woody looked grim. "Yeah, and they left us with a mess too."

"I see it," Jon mourned. "Renee's chocolate cake is only a black smudge in the sand, and Mum's beach blanket is on fire."

"I wouldn't worry about a cake or a blanket," Tara said primly. "Your mum will just be glad we're all all right."

"And to think," Renee said whimsically, "that I spent all afternoon baking that cake."

They all gazed sadly at the dark glob of goo mixed into the golden sand before Woody sighed dismally. "Our party's ruined, so I guess we may as well go home."

Gloomily, they all echoed his decision, doused the fire, gathered what was left of their things and said a sad goodnight.

Twenty yards apart, though, Woody called over his shoulder, "Hey, Jon! I'm going out on the boat with Dad in the morning to check his lobster traps. He said it's okay for you to come if you want. We leave at five o'clock."

Jon cupped his hands around his mouth and called back, "Sure, thanks, I'll set my alarm clock."

Tara felt a pang of disappointment that she had not been invited. But, then, perhaps the boat wasn't big enough for so many people.

Jon was so thankful that the truth about Tara being his aunt was out in the open and that nobody cared, he felt almost giddy with relief. The, sensing Tara's feelings, he said softly, "The boat is small. Besides,

Woody told me that too many people on board get in the way."

"It's all right," she replied easily. "Renee and I will find something to do." Brightening, she added, "Maybe we'll bake another chocolate cake."

Jon's brown eyes slid over to her in the darkness. "You don't know how to cook."

Tara's eyes twinkled. "I can make macaroni and cheese and potato salad. That's cooking. But I have to admit my mother was always too busy to teach me much." Defending herself, she said wistfully, "But I do want to learn, so maybe Renee will teach me."

A light grey fog was rolling in just as they got to the house. They found Jon's mother and father sitting in front of the television watching the news.

Mrs Rogers looked up in surprise when she realized they had only a few things in a basket and no beach blanket. "Back so soon?"

Dismally, the kids sat down to relate the night's events. But the further they got into the story the more Mr And Mrs Rogers showed their alarm.

"And then," Tara said, ending the story on a note of triumph, "just as Renee and I were being dragged to their boat, a woman in a long black dress came out on the widow's walk of that tower and frightened the boys away." With a story she considered well told, she sat back with her arms folded across her chest.

"What do you make of that, Mum?" Jon asked eagerly, still refusing to speak to his dad unless it was absolutely necessary.

But it was his father who answered. "I have no idea what or who you saw on that old tower, but I assure you it was not Evangeline Hawkins!"

Jon clenched his jaw and remained silent. Tara, sensing the tension between her nephew and her brother, glanced uneasily from one to the other.

Wearing a black frown, Jon persisted, "Mum? What do you think?"

Mrs Rogers, too, looked troubled. "Your father has already answered you, and I agree with him. Right now I just feel very thankful that the two of you are safe."

Jon's father reached for the telephone. "I'm alerting the authorities to what happened." After reporting the incident, he murmured, "Oh really? Good. Yes. Thanks very much."

Both Tara and Jon had been listening intently, and now Tara asked, "What is it, Fred?"

"Seems those three boys were causing trouble in town, too. They were caught and locked up half-an-hour ago."

The harsh ringing of Jon's alarm clock screamed through his room promptly at twenty minutes to five. His first thought was to strangle it, but then he remembered why it was so cruelly waking him and he tore out of bed. Quickly he slipped into his clothes, snatched a piece of toast and a small bottle of orange juice and was off to meet Woody and his dad.

Tara, though, slept on until seven-thirty, when she woke up to brilliant sunlight falling across her face. After a quick shower, she ate some toast and scrambled eggs, saw that the fog had been dispelled and started down the beach to the lighthouse to find her new friend. However, Renee was on her way to find Tara and the two met in front of the famous haunted house.

"No sign of Evangeline this morning," Renee reported lightly.

"You know," Tara mused, "it's all kind of strange. But when you look at the place in bright sunshine it doesn't look quite as threatening, do you think?"

Renee smoothed back her hair and grinned impishly, "Want to explore it?"

Tara bit her lip, taken aback at the words. "I don't know. I think Jon and Woody had a pretty scary night when they stayed there, and I doubt if Jonathon is much afraid of anything."

Renee stood with her hands resting on her narrow hips, thinking hard. "Maybe we can prove that girls are braver than boys."

"I don't know," Tara said again. "If you will remember, we did see that mysterious woman up there on the tower last night."

Renee lifted an eyebrow. "Yes, but she didn't try to hurt us, she only protected us."

Still feeling reluctant, Tara admitted meekly, "That's true, isn't it."

While they were talking, they had without realizing it walked closer and closer to the great three-storey house. The sandstone tower shone red and innocent in the morning light.

Grasping the latch on the front door, Renee tugged. It was stuck. "Let's go into the house from the tower. Woody told me about a small door there that leads inside the house."

Furtively now, the girls crept toward the door leading into the tower. There, though the door grudgingly ground against the sand, it opened easily enough. A rush of cool, dank air rushed out at them, along with the smells of a hundred-year-old house.

Tara shivered. No wonder Evangeline had needed an upstairs room where she could work! "It's so cold and dark in here and…" She stopped speaking as some faint flutter of sound caught her ear. "Did you hear that?"

Renee was frowning and rigid. "Wind," she hissed. "It had to be the wind."

Then without warning, the sound of a baby crying came from farther away. It was a pitiful, lonely sound that caused the girls to clutch one another in fear.

Tara mouthed the words, "Oh no!"

Renee shuddered. "I've always heard that at certain times you can hear a baby crying, but I guess I never really believed it till now."

Tara tried to think logically. "Renee, I told my brother what happened last night, about us seeing Evangeline there and all. Fred says it definitely was not Evangeline." Her breath caught in her throat before she challenged. "So I say we go up there and find out what's going on."

If Tara had suggested they leap off the widow's walk, her words would have been no less startling. Renee visibly drew back. Her mouth dropped open and she clutched her hands in terror. "Listen, Tara, I've accepted Jesus as my Saviour, and I know He promised to take care of us, but...well, I don't know if He'd protect us if we do something really stupid."

Tara's mouth twisted to one side for a long thoughtful moment. Then, her dimples winking in and out, she said, "How can it be stupid to want to find the truth? Like you said, whoever was on the widow's walk last night protected us, they didn't try to hurt us."

"Oh you're probably right," Renee admitted grudgingly. "Okay, then, I guess if you're brave enough to go up there, then I ought to be, too." Pressing her lips into a firm, determined line she added, "Let's go."

Tara giggled as they tiptoed up the first four steps. "I wonder what the boys will say when they find out we explored the whole tower?"

Renee turned with a half smile. "What if they don't believe us? Maybe they'll think we're making it up."

"We'll try and find some kind of proof to take back with us," Tara announced promptly. "Something from the room upstairs."

But in spite of their brave words, they were trembling with dread and excitement. Holding the rusted iron railing with cold hands, they inched their way upwards. Five steps from the top, just as their heads were about to pop through the room once reserved for Evangeline's artwork, they stopped cold.

Eyes wide with stunned amazement, the colour ebbing from their faces, they stood dumbfounded. For a figure had just flitted past their eyes and disappeared into thin air!

Lobster Boat

The fishing-boat staggered drunkenly through the oncoming waves. Salt spray lashed Jon's face and coated his glasses until he was constantly taking them off to dry them. Droplets of salt water lingered on his dark hair, glistening in the sunlight like silver tears.

Suddenly the boat slowed and came to a stop, bobbing unsteadily in the water. Woody's father leaned over the side of the boat to do something.

"What's happening?" Jon asked curiously.

Woody smiled and gestured. "Dad's bringing up a lobster trap to see if he caught anything."

Jon discovered that he was watching with interest as a large wire trap was lifted from the water. "Looks like he got one, all right!"

Woody grunted with satisfaction. "A big one, too. Now watch this, Jon." Woody expertly snapped rubber bands around the lobster's pincers to protect him from being harmed.

Jon frowned at the trap. "Why does the trap have different compartments?"

"I'll show you," Woody replied breezily. "See here? That's the kitchen."

Jon's mouth fell open. "Kitchen?"

"Right. And over here, that's the side entrance where the lobster enters the trap. It comes into the kitchen, takes the bait from the spike right there and then, when it tries to get out, it finds itself trapped in the bedroom."

"Fantastic," Jon breathed in awe. "So lobster traps have rooms just like a house."

"Pretty much." Woody smiled with pride. "When we take them out of the bedroom we put rubber bands around their pincers so we can handle them. After that, we ice them down."

Jon looked out over the endless expanse of blue-green water, then swung his gaze back to the boat. "Then what?"

"Then Dad takes them into town and sells them to a supermarket or to a restaurant. Sometimes to tourists who want the freshest lobsters." Woody's brows lifted. "Of course Dad makes more money by selling them to tourists."

"Sure, I can see that." Jon heaved a sigh and leaned on the boat's railing. This was really kind of interesting, being out on the boat and learning about lobstering first hand. In a way he did like the smell of the ocean. The constant motion of the boat probably could get into a person's blood. Not, of course, that it was for him! But for today it did seem pleasant out on the water and feeling the sun and salt spray on his face.

"Are you going to stay in town while your dad sells the lobsters?" Jon had decided to walk on back to the house if Woody remained in town.

"Not today," Woody replied and passed a hand over his damp sandy hair. "We can walk back home if you want. It's not that far. Just three miles."

Jon wiped his glasses free of salt water again. "I'd like to go on back." Grinning half-heartedly he added, "We'll find out what the girls have been up to."

Woody laughed knowingly. "They're probably doing girl stuff, like baking biscuits. I hope they're baking chocolate chip cookies. That would be really cool."

Jon watched the sparkling wake the boat was leaving behind. "It must be really boring to be a girl. I don't see how they stand it."

"That's for sure," Woody murmured gravely.

"Woody?"

"Yeah?"

"Look back there on the rocks. Don't I see our man out there again?"

Woody peered closely. "Yeah, you're right, Jon! But what's the big attraction anyway?"

Tara and Renee stood paralyzed on the steps of the ancient tower. They had both glimpsed the fleeting figure, and it had not been a ghost!

Quietly and cautiously, they backed down the stairs. Three steps from the bottom they stopped to listen, but they neither saw nor heard anything else.

Two steps from the bottom they took a flying leap into space and shot out of the door like rockets. Only when they were again enveloped by warm sunlight did they stop to look back.

Her teeth rattling, Renee said dryly, "Well, I g-guess we won't b-be exploring th-that house today."

Tara's grey eyes were wild and filled with panic. She didn't stop wailing until the creaming waves were washing over her feet. "I guess not."

"B-but you know what?" Renee went on doggedly. "The Hawkins' ghosts could still live there. But I'm positive someone else does too. Because I know that what we saw was real, a real person."

Tara nodded in silent agreement. "I only caught a glimpse, but you're right: it was real. Oh, but Renee, none of this makes any sense."

Renee's long legs refused to hold her up, so she slid down onto the warm sand and let her hands drop loosely in her lap. "I feel like we're playing a part in some weird game and we don't know who the other players are." Lifting a limp hand, she plucked off the characters on her fingers one at a time. "There's that strange man on the rocks who looks like he's watching the house. Then there's the person who seems to be Evangeline. The boys have seen Captain Hawkins, so he has to be one of the characters in this crazy plot."

Tara broke in with, "But I saw the captain, too, remember?"

Renee's freckles scrunched up in a brooding frown. "That's right, I forgot about that. Okay, and we heard the baby crying, so that's another character."

"But who did we see in the tower, and how did they disappear like that?"

Renee pulled her knees up and stared at the sand through them, as though she might find the answer written there. "Boy, don't I wish I knew!"

Neither of them spoke for a while, and then Tara said hesitantly, "Renee?"

Renee looked at her with a faint smile, waiting.

"I'm beginning to like it here. You know? Like it's really home." When Renee nodded her understanding, Tara went on slowly. "But Jon's having a rough time with it. He'd lived in Colorado all his life and all his friends were there, so it's pretty hard for him. So far he hates it here. I wonder…would you mind helping me pray that he'll adjust somehow?"

Renee promised solemnly, "I will." She did not add how she had heard the resentment and bitterness in Jon's voice whenever his father was mentioned. "I just know," she added gently, "that God will help him."

Tara picked up a small stick and made aimless designs in the sand. "I've known Jon all my life, since we were babies, really, and he was always a strong Christian until we moved…" She didn't complete the sentence but said instead, "Thanks, Renee, for praying, and thanks for understanding."

Half-turning, she stared up at the salt-encrusted windows of the tower. "If there is someone up there, he must really keep low so he can't be seen."

Renee scrambled to her feet gingerly. "You know what? There has to be another window on the back wall of the tower." Pushing up her chin with a finger, she added thoughtfully, "I remember walking around there a couple of times, but I'm not sure."

Tara's dark eyes narrowed. "Let's go and find out. As long as we don't get too close, that is." She blew out her breath in exasperation. "Don't you just hate it that we're afraid to explore the house without the boys?"

Renee giggled and swept her hair behind her ears. "Yes, but remember, they were afraid too. Maybe the four of us should go in there together and snoop around."

They chose a wide path around the tower before stopping. The lofty structure still had a certain majesty about it, even after so many years. With its white pillars supporting the porch, the house could still be a beautiful place, not a mansion for the dark world of ghosts.

"I'm surprised the windows aren't all broken out," Tara remarked.

Renee shrugged. "That's because the last people who lived here planned to turn it into an inn or a museum or something and replaced the ones that were broken."

Tara gazed at her new friend earnestly. "What happened?"

"Same old thing. The weird noises began and the people up and abandoned it."

Tara pressed her lips and sighed. "I can understand that." She remembered what her brother had said about buying the house and converting it into an inn.

Renee was standing still, examining the upper part of the tower. "No window," she reported in a puzzled voice.

Tara bit the inside of her cheek. "Doesn't that seem kind of odd? You'd think Evangeline would have needed all the light she could get."

"You'd think so," Renee agreed slowly. "But suppose there's a secret room up there? After all, when this place was built, there were pirates and robbers. Sometimes houses were looted and the people inside killed. And remember, Captain Hawkins was away at sea a lot, so surely he would have made certain there was a place for his wife and his servants to hide. Sure! History says the captain was a kind and caring man, so he would have made sure they had a place to be safe."

"That's true," Tara said, frowning.

Renee folded her arms, thinking it all over. "So whoever we saw in the upper room of this tower that disappeared so fast must have discovered the secret room and dived into it!"

A Black Dress

Jon and Woody walked down the beach with a long, easy gait. The lobster catch had been excellent and Woody's father was doing a profitable business. The boys had said their goodbyes, grabbed sandwiches and soft drinks at a nearby deli and left town.

A short distance from the lighthouse, Woody stopped and grabbed Jon's arm. "Pssst! See out there on the rocks? Our man is still there and don't tell me he's fishing!"

Jon paused as Woody pretended to be examining a piece of driftwood. "I wasn't going to, because I don't think he's fishing either. But there he is, all hunkered down, doing something. I'll bet when we get in front of the old house we won't be able to see him."

"Uh-huh," Woody growled. "But he'll be watching it all the same."

They continued on their way and tried to put the odd man on the rocks out of their minds.

"It's too bad the girls couldn't have come with us today," Jon said, sounding a little wistful. "Tara's always so interested in learning new things, she would have loved hearing you tell about the lobster traps and everything."

Woody picked up a piece of driftwood, tested it with his carving knife, then flung it away and tucked the knife back into the waistband of his jeans. "You really care about her, don't you?"

Jon's eyes widened with surprise. Making a careless gesture with his hands, he said reluctantly, "Well, I – I guess maybe I do. A little, anyway."

Woody grinned impishly. "Hey, it's okay to like your relatives!"

Jon's laugh was weak and unsure. "I just hope they made the chocolate chip cookies we talked about."

Before Woody could answer, there was a squeal of delight, and they saw the girls racing toward them like they were being chased by Captain Hawkins' ghost.

"Hi," Woody called. "So did you bake chocolate chip cookies?"

"Did we bake what?" Renee demanded tartly. "What are you talking about?"

Disappointed, Woody blurted out, "You mean you girls haven't been in the house baking biscuits for us?"

Renee's look was withering. "You're kidding, right? What we've been doing is detective work."

"That's right," Tara put in indignantly. "We've been exploring that old house."

Woody's shoulders slumped and he looked at the house warily. "You didn't."

"We didn't exactly explore the house" Tara said quickly, correcting herself, "because we didn't get that far. But we did explore some of the tower."

"We're pretty sure we found out something important," Renee reported eagerly. "We think maybe there's a secret room in the upstairs part!" In her enthusiasm she began to ramble. "See, there's no window on the back wall of the tower, and with robbers and pirates around in those days, Evangeline and her servants would have needed a place to hide, and oh! I think it would be the coolest thing ever if we could find it!"

When she finally stopped long enough to gulp in a breath of air, Tara took over. "We'd like you guys to come with us –"

Jon threw up both hands in protest. "Will you both slow down and tell us what you're talking about?"

Confused, the girls stared at each other. What was wrong with the boys? They had made themselves perfectly clear.

"Okay," Tara agreed, trying to sound calm and in control. "We went inside the tower to scout around. Then we were going to go into the house –"

Jon's brown eyes behind his glasses were solemn. "Only you didn't."

"We meant to, but first we went up in the tower to see what was there."

"That's when we saw someone, a figure, flit by and disappear," Renee finished excitedly.

Woody's brow darkened. "Just like before."

Jon was trying to deal with this news, but he did wish those screaming, shrieking gulls would shut up so he could really tune in on what the girls were saying.

"Anyway," Tara continued briskly, "we went around to the back of the tower to find out if we could see anyone through the rear window, and guess what?"

"Not a clue," Woody replied dryly.

Tara nodded triumphantly. "We saw nothing. Nothing at all, and do you know why? Because there's no window there."

Unable to help herself, Renee cut in. "That's why we think there's a secret room up there in the tower."

"But wouldn't pirates have guessed that, too," Woody suggested drolly.

"Why would they?" Tara asked ruefully. "Besides, even if they did suspect a hidden room, how would they ever have found it?"

"So we think," Renee persisted brightly, "that the man who has been coming to those rocks all the time found the secret room and is staying there at night. And I think he's still there."

Woody picked up another piece of driftwood, examined it with a critical eye, shook his head and flung it away. "Sis, I sure hate to blow holes in your theory, but that man is out on the rocks right this minute, so it wasn't him you saw."

Jon pulled his baseball cap from his head and studied it intently. Replacing it, he said, "Woody's right. We both saw him. He's crouched down out of sight from here, but I do think he's watching this old house through binoculars."

Disappointed that they had been proved wrong, Tara breathed lamely, "How weird."

A brisk wind was kicking up, blowing sand and causing the waves to grow high and choppy. Down the beach from them, breakers lashed the headland with fury. Dark clouds lurked on the horizon.

"We kept waiting for you guys to come back so we could get in the house together," Renee confessed reluctantly. "We're really curious now, but, honest, we don't want to go in there by ourselves."

Her words caused the boys to puff out their chests a little and square their shoulders. What in the world would girls do without boys to help and protect them? Okay. It was time to prove their manhood, be bold and courageous.

Swaggering with pride, they led the way straight back to the tower, opened the door and stepped inside. The girls followed along like furtive shadows, their eyes darting through the gloomy interior as they searched for anything unusual.

Jon removed his cap and put it on backwards as he boldly led the way up the narrow spiral stairs. "Okay now," he growled, sounding crisp and businesslike. "We'll go up here first and take a look around. Surely we can tell by the size of the room if there's a secret hiding place."

Woody played along like a real trooper. "Sure, and after that we'll go inside the house and explore every single room." His chin lifted with determination. "If there's foul work afoot," he went on, beginning to sound like a detective in a mystery book, "we are going to find it."

Outside the tower, clouds had crowded out the sunlight, but the interior of the tower was so dim anyway that no one noticed. A howling gale was busy rearranging the sandy beach and blowing a mound of sand against the front door of the old house.

Three-quarters of the way up the stairs they all stopped dead still. Somewhere, a baby was crying frantically! The sound was chilling, and even the boys lost their bravado and began to tremble.

"There's that baby again!" Tara hissed. "We heard that before, too."

"The Hawkins baby," Woody ground out balefully.

"But how is that possible?" Jon protested softly. He was still unsure about ghosts. "That baby died soon after it was born, you said so yourself, Woody."

"Yeah, well, there it is, anyway" Woody said grimly. His teeth were clenched and his muscles bunched up as he tried to put on a confidence he did not feel. After all, there were girls here to impress!

Jon, too, was trembling on the inside, still trying to make himself look confident. He continued on up the stairs and stepped into the tower's upper room. The girls, making an effort to mask their fear, followed him.

The crying baby stopped as though someone had picked it up to comfort it. A moment later, however, it was crying as wildly as before. But at least the organ was quiet, an enormous old dust-covered instrument that sat cowering on the left side of the room. Some of the knobs were missing and it looked totally abandoned. Canvasses, remnants of Evangeline's work, were stacked against one wall.

The girls centred their attention on the rear wall where a window should have been. A blank wall met their gaze, just as it had when they had searched the back of the tower from the ground.

"See there!" Renee exclaimed piously. "All the walls are made of sandstone, but only three sides have windows in them. I know there's a secret room behind this back wall!"

Woody was already pushing the wall and studying it. "If there is, I don't see any way to get inside."

"I've been thinking about that," Tara brooded gloomily. "And…well, maybe we don't even want to. I mean, if someone really is hiding out in there –"

Jonathon took off his cap again and twirled it on a finger. "Don't you think" he suggested, "that if there's a secret room here, there may be others inside the house too? If pirates or other robbers came to loot the house, Evangeline and her servants would never have had time to go to the tower and up the stairs to the hidden room from here." He spread his arms. "Maybe there's even some connection from the house into the upper part of the tower. Sure! That's got to be it!"

Woody nodded, one brow cocked. "That makes a lot of sense. So let's forget this tower and go and explore the house. I mean, really explore it."

The fellows turned back toward the stairs, but Tara was still studying the interior of this strange room. Suddenly she cried shrilly, "Well, just look at what I found!"

The others turned back slowly and without much interest, but Renee had detected the astonishment in Tara's voice and spun around.

Tara was standing on one side of the room fingering something. "Remember when we saw that person in the long black dress on the widow's walk? Well," she quipped, "I just found the dress!"

What she was looking at was a long black dress, ancient and tattered, hanging on a hook. "Here's the dress and for sure it's not a ghost! Someone in this place was wearing that dress to frighten away those awful boys."

The Crying Baby

The other kids crowded around Tara to stare at the black dress. It hung there on a wall peg like a tired and depressed old soul. There was no doubt but that it had belonged to another time. It had a high neck and long sleeves and somehow had held together all these years.

"I'll bet it was packed away somewhere and someone found it," Woody said, nodding.

"But it did belong to Evangeline Hawkins," Renee drawled whimsically. "I guess she had more than one, because she was wearing a black dress when she leaped off the widow's walk." Looking very wise, she added softly, "At least that's how the story goes."

Jon's fists were driven deeply into his pockets and his mouth was twisted to one side. "Then there really is someone living in this old house!" Withdrawing one hand, he quickly pushed up his glasses. "Playing the organ and making all sorts of noises to scare people away."

Woody chewed his lip, thinking hard. "Yes, but these noises have been going on ever since the Hawkins lived here, they didn't just start."

Jon nodded. "Good point."

Renee's blue eyes were still troubled. "Well, all I know is that whoever is living here now scared those boys away."

As though this conversation had been overheard, there came again the eerie, faraway sound of a baby crying wildly. Its small voice lifted and fell in despair, then broke off into strangled sobs.

"I don't know about any of this," Woody offered dolefully.

"Just listen to that!" Tara said with a shiver. "It gives me the creeps."

"It's coming from somewhere above us," Jon reported.

"Of course," Renee agreed quickly. "That's because all the bedrooms are on the upper floors, and that means the baby's room would have been up there too."

Tara blew out her breath impatiently. Hands on her hips, she challenged, "Okay, I don't know about the rest of you, but I'm all for going upstairs to track down that crying baby."

"You're not serious?" Renee asked in astonishment.

"Oh, you just watch me! I'm tired of being chased away from this place by so-called ghosts. Now that the four of us are together, it doesn't feel nearly as scary as it did before."

Jon lifted his chin a notch and squared his shoulders, trying to look macho. If the girls were willing to risk their necks investigating this old mansion, then he could certainly prove his manhood! Giving Woody a brief nod, he cried recklessly, "All right then, let's go and explore the upstairs of the house!"

Woody was right behind him as he scrambled down the tower stairs. "At least we're pretty sure now that there really is a secret room."

"Yes," said Renee primly, "only we still have no idea how to get into it."

"We will," her brother promised. "I think we're starting to unravel some of the mysteries now."

They slipped through the narrow door leading into the house, and after a short inspection of the lower floor, they went directly to the grand, winding staircase.

"Jon, you know something?" Tara gushed. "If my brother gets serious about turning this old place into an inn, he could do an awful lot with it."

"Oh, right," Jon hooted, "that's all we need, another reason to stay here." The raw bitterness swept through him once more, engulfing him like the crashing breakers out on the rocks. His dad was so wrong to make him leave his home and his friends for some weird house on a beach! Even though this adventure actually did spark a little excitement in him.

They roamed through a number of bedrooms on the second floor but could not trace the sound of the crying baby. Now, added to the sobbing were the deep, desperate moans of a man in anguish.

Tara shivered. "Well, I sure don't see a baby's room anywhere."

They explored every single room. Most of them were empty, the furniture having been carried away years before by looters. What little remained was broken and tattered and covered by long years of dust. Sand had forced its way through every crack and crevice, leaving tiny piles of the golden stuff on every windowsill.

"The baby was sick," Woody pointed out, "So probably Evangeline would have kept it in her room. But just remember the people who tried to live here after the Hawkins may have got rid of the baby furniture that had been in the house then."

"I didn't think of that," Tara admitted ruefully.

Jon was busy tapping walls and searching for clues to a hidden room. "I don't know," he sighed, "if there's a secret room on this floor I can't imagine where it could be."

Renee had a large smudge of dirt on her face that hid the freckles. The fingers of one hand wrapped around her chin, she announced briskly, "The servant's quarters would have been on the third floor, and that's just about the same height as the tower. Maybe that's where it is."

"Let's find out," Jon muttered and started away to find the stairs leading to the third floor. The sound of the crying baby was suddenly so close to him that he was struck dumb. "Boy! Just when I've convinced myself that there's no such thing as ghosts, that baby starts crying again!"

Tara took a firm stand. "I know what we're hearing, and I know all about the organ playing and the footsteps when no one is there, but I'll still have to be convinced that ghosts are real."

Woody gave her a sharp, troubled look and turned off the wide hallway toward the steep staircase that would take them to the third floor. He asked quietly, "Aren't you forgetting that you saw the captain's face? Scar and all! I mean, what does it take to make you believe?"

Tara bit her lip and could find no words with which to reply.

"I never saw him," Renee announced piously.

"Well, the rest of us did." Woody insisted. "And he wasn't part of our imagination either! He was real!"

"I know, and I have to admit that's pretty weird," Tara agreed reluctantly. "But no matter how things look, the Bible still doesn't say anything about ghosts."

At mention of the Bible, Jon was hit by a surge of conviction. How long had it been since he had taken time to read his Bible all by himself? He clenched his jaw and glanced at Woody. Yeah, he was a pretty rotten testimony to him, too.

"Well, I think – " Woody stopped speaking as he opened the door leading to the narrow stairway. "Ah-hah! Come on, everybody, let's go up there and see what we can find."

No one objected, and Jon put aside his troubled thoughts. He was positive, though, that he would never have peace in his heart again.

It felt much safer exploring the house now that the four of them were together. Eager and excited, they wanted only to continue their investigation.

However, they had been so engrossed in exploring that they had not noticed the storm that had moved in. Until now, that is. The wind had whipped itself into a frenzy squawking and shrieking through unseen cracks and howling down the chimneys. Soot and dust went flying from the several fireplaces. Rain slashed the windowpanes and slid down them in muddy rivers. Waves crashed on shore, while gulls took refuge in the rocks and hid their heads beneath their wings.

"Well," said Renee breathlessly, "if Evangeline and her baby had to hide in some secret room on the third floor, they sure would have had trouble getting to it on time."

Woody promptly disagreed. "Oh I don't know. Maybe the servants went into the room from the third floor and Evangeline had some way of getting inside it through the downstairs."

After a puffing minute-and-a-half, they reached the lofty third floor of the house, where they stood gasping for breath. The booming thunder was louder now and they saw through the windows that sharp daggers of lightning were stabbing their way through the dark clouds.

"This place is almost soundproof," Jon offered and wiped the perspiration from his forehead with the back of his hand. "I had no idea it was storming like this."

Woody's grin was impish. "What more could we ask for? An old haunted house complete with all sorts of weird noises, and on top of that, a raging storm." He looked around warily and asked cheerfully, "Shall we?"

Two bay windows sat out from the second floor, and the first floor seemed sprawling and enormous, but here on the third floor the house was smaller. Their voices when they spoke were hollow and empty-sounding. The rooms were also empty and smelled strongly of mould and age. Wallpaper had been shredded from the walls by the sharp teeth of mice in need of material for their nests.

Renee shuddered. "It smells awful."

In one narrow back room they discovered a cluttered pile of boards and rolls of wallpaper, now half-eaten by mice. It seemed that the captain had planned to add some more to the house and that the tragedies had ended those plans. It was there that Tara made a discovery.

"Well, well," she droned triumphantly, "just take a look at this."

The others crowded around instantly to see what she had found. It was a crushed Styrofoam cup half buried under one of the boards. "I guess our ghost likes coffee," Woody observed dryly. "He's getting a little sloppy if you ask me."

Immediately his words were punctuated by a shrill scream. Then the baby was crying in agony.

The Secret Room

The plaintive cry brought the four kids back into a huddle, where they stared about them in confusion and dread.

"Just don't try and tell me that's not a baby crying" Woody croaked, "because that's exactly what it is."

Outside the house, the wind shrieked and howled like a mad monster on the loose. They weren't sure which was worse, the screaming infant or the wind. The whole house seemed to quake and shudder under the impact of the storm. And something banged frantically against the side of the house.

"Some storm," Tara said, her voice breaking. Her smoky eyes were wide with fright in a face the colour of paste.

"That Hawkins baby must have been in terrible pain before it died," Renee put in sadly.

Jon dragged his thoughts back from all the guilt and frustration he was feeling. "Well, all I can say is, whoever is living in this place is not a ghost, because ghosts don't drink coffee and eat sandwiches. That much I'm positive about!" Whoever is living here is getting really sloppy to leave a Styrofoam cup behind."

"I think he tried to hide it under the boards," Renee announced importantly, "and that some mouse dragged it out again."

Woody jumped in with, "I think the guy just forgot about it."

Tara picked up the cup by its rim and studied it like it was scientific evidence. Shrugging, she noted, "Yes, but look: the cup is old and dirty. It seems to me that it could have been left here by some beach bum who came to spend the night."

Renee, eager to explain away some of the evidence, said primly, "That's right, Tara! A beach bum could have wandered in here and spent the night. He could have brought food from town. He wouldn't have had a reason to try and hide anything."

A fierce rumble of thunder rattled the windows, startling them. Wind whooshed down the chimneys like it was coming in after them. Forked tongues of lightning flickered in and out. One minute the rooms were brilliantly lighted and the next they were dark and gloomy. Right now the damp, smelly old place was beginning to feel more sinister that ever, with its crying baby, its secret whisperings and moanings, and the footsteps that sounded when no one was there.

"I don't much like this house," she reported meekly and hoped the others would agree.

"Aw, nothing can hurt us as long as we're together," Woody comforted. "Besides, we can't go out there in that storm." He went to a window and peered outside. "Take a look. It's raining like crazy and the fog's starting to come in."

Renee looked over her brother's shoulder. "Woody's right, we wouldn't stand a ghost of a chance out there right now." She hesitated then added wryly, "Excuse the word ghost."

Jon's grin was lopsided. "I guess our spy out there on the rocks is soaked by now." Suddenly he frowned, realizing how long it had been since he had seen anything worth smiling about.

"Look," Woody said briskly, "as long as we've come this far, and since we can't get home right now anyway, let's go ahead and check out the rest of this floor. After all," he added almost reproachfully, "we haven't looked very hard for the secret room from up here."

Jon's sigh was ragged. "I guess you're right." His eyes swept the area. "Okay, we already know there isn't a hidden room along the outside walls where there are windows because there's no room for one." He thought for a moment. "But there are a few small rooms we haven't explored. So…Tara, why don't you and Renee take the ones on the left and Woody and I will go on back to the smaller rooms and take a look.

Be sure," he instructed, "to tap on the walls to see if any of them sound hollow."

Renee's frown was dark and questioning, "but what if there really is someone living here and we get him all irritated and upset by our snooping around?"

Woody heaved his shoulders. "He may not be here right now, sis. Or he could be in the tower." He grabbed the sides of his head and complained bitterly, "I wish that baby would stop crying!"

It was maddening. The shrieking would let up for a minute or two and start in all over again, sometimes more frantic that before, and the moaning was nearly deafening. Then, suddenly, from faraway, the organ began to play. Its low, mournful bass keys droned even into the area where the four stricken kids cowered all over again.

"I'm telling you," Tara said balefully, "I don't like it here!" Just in case anyone was interested. "Renee, let's stick really close together while we look in those other rooms."

Renee's freckles stood out in dark splotches against her pale face. Looking nervous and unsure, she croaked, "That's fine by me! I don't want to be by myself in this awful place!"

The girls went off one way to prowl through the small bedroom where the cook had made her home, while Woody vanished into another small room near the back of the house. Jon sneezed from all the dust, wiped his glasses and headed for the very back room, which appeared to have been used to store linens and cleaning supplies.

"Hmmm," he mused. "This might have possibilities. The problem is, now I'm not positive which way the tower is from here. "I think…yes, it's got to be to my left."

A soft thumping sound alerted him and he froze, tense and wide-eyed. Of course he had heard weird banging noises before, so this really wasn't anything new.

He hit his head against one of the shelves, rubbed the spot until the pain eased away, then began to carefully tap the walls with his knuckles.

"Whoa!" he cried in a whisper. "Hold on a minute there!" He backtracked a little and tapped again. The panel had a different sound to it. "Yes sir, I just may have found something." Gently he rapped again. "It does sound different. But I'll make sure before I tell the others."

Thumping the wall from the height of his shoulder to his knees, he discovered that the entire panel appeared to be hollow. It was narrow, though, barely wide enough for a grown man to press through. Kneeling, his fingers explored every square inch of the wall panel. There must be some sort of device that would release the panel into the secret room.

"I want to make sure," he told himself ruefully.

The portion of wall slid inside itself so unexpectedly that afterwards Jon was never sure just what the release had been. But there it was, the hidden room was right in front of him, an area filled with cobwebs, dust and the smell of dry wood. It was as black as the inside of that old mine shaft he had explored back in Colorado that time.

Congratulating himself for his cleverness, he decided to take a quick look inside before making his discovery known to the others. His light picked up a narrow passage, then three steps that led upwards into the dark unknown.

"Must lead to the tower," he mused.

He was already up the steps when he realized with a shock that the wall panel was sliding quietly back into position. At the moment he was a prisoner between two walls, where bits of plaster crunched under his shoes. Thoroughly alarmed, he spun around in the close quarters and would have rushed back to yell for help, when a powerful hand was clamped over his mouth and he was dragged back helplessly into the secret tower room.

Man with a
Bulldog Face

Wild-eyed and struggling fiercely, Jon was calmly
hauled into a long, narrow room without a
window. In his frantic state of mind, he knew only
dimly that he was somewhere in either the tower
or the rear of the third floor of the house. He was
completely helpless against the man's brute strength,
a prisoner in the hands of – what? A criminal? A
madman? Certainly not a ghost!

What stunned him most was that this was not the
man who had looked in the tower window at him.
Neither was it the man Tara had met in the graveyard.
This man was short and square, built like a box, and
his face looked squeezed together like a bulldog's. His

hair was light brown and thinning, and he had not seen a barber in a very long time. But it was the man's eyes that trapped Jon like a rabbit facing the hunter. They looked dead and cold as a rattler's, and he had no scar!

"Calm down, kid, or I'll have to do something we'll both be sorry for!" the stranger hissed against Jon's ear.

His heart crashing like the thunder outside the house, his pulse a runaway freight train, Jon tried to make himself relax. He was too young to die. Much as he hated his new home, he wasn't anxious to go to heaven just yet, and this guy sure looked like he meant what he said.

In spite of the man's square toughness, he was wiry and could move very fast. Almost before Jon knew what was happening, there was a slab of duct tape over his mouth and his wrists and ankles were bound. Helpless and terrified, he lay against the wall struggling. Afraid Jon would kick the wall and alert the others, the man lifted him as if he were a feather pillow, and placed him away from the wall.

Making muffled sounds behind the tape, Jon asked what was going to happen to him.

The man's grin was smirking and evil, Jon decided, and did not have any humour in it. "You just be nice and quiet," Bulldog Face said in a whisper. "You can't talk so don't try. If you're a good boy, I'll allow you to live. It's like this, see: you are either my ticket out of here alive or I'll have to leave you here to be found later. Let's make it the first thing, shall we?"

The word 'later' had a most ominous ring to it. If Jon were left here alone, he would probably be dead before he was ever found. Right here, in this lonely, isolated, hidden room that no one knew about but him.

Dear Lord Jesus, he prayed, please, I don't want to die. It was the first time he realized with a shock, that he had prayed from his heart in a very long while. Please, please help me. Show somebody where I am.

His prayers were selfish and self-centred, but he was too terrified to know or even care. At least he was smart enough to know that if God did not come to his rescue he was a goner.

Bulldog Face was doing something in the small room and Jon twisted his head up off the floor to look. His flashlight had been turned off and a single candle lit the space. He saw now that the room was cluttered with empty Styrofoam cups and plastic sandwich wrappers, so evidently the man had been hiding out here for some time. Then he saw what the man was up to. He had unsheathed a mean looking snub-nosed .38, which lay in his lap. At his side was another weapon, a wicked-appearing hunting knife.

Yeah, this guy meant business all right.

As though coming from another world and another time, Jon heard the voices of his friends and Tara. Tara. His aunt. No, Tara, his friend and almost, his sister. How he longed to be out there with them.

Bulldog Face also heard the voices and cocked his head, trying to hear what they were saying. Deciding it would be almost impossible for them to discover this hidden room, too, he took a huge bite from a sandwich and washed it down with a swallow of orange juice from a half-gallon carton beside him.

"Sounds like your friends are worried about you," the man sneered. "Too bad, because they won't be able to find you. Even if they should, I could take care of them too." He patted his gun lovingly as one would stroke a pet dog.

Jon wiggled, trying to make himself more comfortable, and saw that the walls of his prison were sandstone blocks. That meant two things. The room was practically soundproof. The perfect place to hide from pirates in the olden days, and it meant that he was in the tower.

Then in the flickering, weaving candlelight, he saw something else. Paintings. Several of them were stacked against the wall next to Bulldog Face, and the colours were still as bright as the day they were painted. But of course they would be in this dry, airless place.

Evangeline's paintings, he told himself ruefully. Wow! If Dad actually does buy this place and turn it into an inn, think how much atmosphere it would add to have her paintings hanging on the walls. People would love it!

Whoa! Hold on a minute there. What in the world was he thinking? He hated it here! If his dad bought this place he'd – he'd…

"Jon – a – thon!" It was Tara's shrill, terrified voice and it sounded like it was coming from a long way off.

Bulldog Face kicked Jon's foot and threw him a warning look, then went right on eating as though he was totally unconcerned.

A sob crowded into Jon's throat and misted his eyes. It had been only by accident that he had discovered the opening into this secret room and he still had no idea what the trigger had been that had released the panel. So how in the world could he ever expect his friends to stumble onto it?

Tara and Renee had stuck together like glue as they investigated the bedrooms on the left side of the third floor. But tapping walls and even peering beneath the ancient bed frames told them nothing.

"Well," Renee snorted indignantly, "I know we're on the side of the house where the tower is." She looked over at Tara questioningly. "We are, aren't we?"

Tara nodded, sighed and brushed a dust-covered hand across her face. "We're on the left side, no doubt about that." She gestured. "No windows on this side either, see? That means the tower is smack against the house."

"I think it would have been just awful to occupy a room without a single window," Renee pointed out primly.

Tara combed her hair behind her ears with her hands. "I don't know why we're looking here. There's no secret room."

They followed a thumping sound across the hallway and found Woody industriously tapping the walls and thumping the floor and listening.

"Find anything?" Renee questioned.

Woody jerked his head and a second later let it fall to his chest in defeat. "Not one thing," he answered gloomily. "But we know there has to be a hidden room here somewhere."

"Has Jon found anything?" Tara asked hopefully.

Woody scrambled to his feet. "I don't think so, but we can go find out."

Together they traipsed down the hallway to where Woody had last seen Jonathon. The room was empty.

"Where is he?" Tara asked of no one in particular.

"He must be in another room," Woody reported with confidence. "Hey, Jon, time to give yourself up!"

An ominous silence was his reply.

Quickly now, Woody looked in the other rooms, then headed for the steep, narrow stairs. "He must have gone back down. Come on."

The girls followed, frowning and puzzled.

Tara felt a chill go through her but told herself that was silly. If Jon had gone downstairs, why had he not told them? Dear Lord, she prayed with a quick, anxious look at Renee, let Jon be okay.

But of course he was all right! Why wouldn't he be? Maybe with all the depression he was going through he had gone back home. Sure. Why, right this minute he was probably in his room brooding over the loss of his old friends. The storm had lessened so that would not have been a problem.

They reached the second floor and spread out to look for the missing boy.

Raising her voice a couple of octaves, Tara shouted over and over, "Jon – a – thon! Jon, will you please answer me?"

A cold stillness was her reply.

"Well," Renee stated with authority, "he can't just have vanished. We know he's got to be in here somewhere."

Tara shivered and hugged her arms around her body. Sounding wise and practical, she said, "Maybe not. Maybe he went on back to the house." She glanced at Woody. "You have a watch, what time is it?"

"Twelve-thirty," he answered gravely.

"There you have it, folks," Tara reported sagely, "Jon got hungry and went back home for some lunch."

Woody looked doubtful. "I don't know, that storm was plenty wicked. I think Jon's too smart for that."

Tara flung back her long blonde hair. "But he must have. There's no other answer.'

Woody was still frowning and shaking his head. "Why wouldn't he have told us?"

Since no one could answer that one, they went on back down the great curving staircase to the first floor. There they saw that the rain was almost gone and the sun was trying to push its way through the clouds.

Tara stood at a window and watched while the rain

came to a stop. She was cold and wanted to get out there in the warm sunlight. She was still confident that Jon was right at that moment sitting in the kitchen eating a sandwich.

Where is Jon?

The sun was smiling on a wet, wet world when Tara, Renee and Woody left the tower and went their separate ways. With a breezy, "See you later today!" Tara ran lightly down the long stretch of sand to her new home.

Her hair raced along behind her like a golden streamer and she was humming a new chorus she had learned. She felt blessed to have found a new friend so quickly, and a Christian friend at that. She knew also the odds of that happening were slim, and now Renee was proving to be a trustworthy friend.

"But oh," she said aloud, "I hope Jonathon gets to be real friends with Woody and that he can learn to be happy here."

She lifted her face and gulped in the fresh smell of the sea. Then she watched the screaming, wheeling gulls and smiled at the little sandpipers hopefully poking their beaks into the sand in search of food.

Her gaze lifted then to the great pile of rocks out in the cove where they had so often seen a man who was supposedly fishing. A gasp left her lips. "Can you believe it!" she whispered. "He sure didn't waste any time getting out there after the storm let up!"

It was amazing, but again, Tara knew that if she were standing directly in front of the haunted house the man would be invisible.

She shook her head wonderingly. "He might as well build a house and live there. But why does he come there all the time? What's he after?"

What, indeed? If he was actually fishing he certainly did not seem very serious about it.

"Oh well," she told herself with a shrug, "It's none of my business."

Once more her feet took wings as she ran up the porch steps and burst through the door singing out, "Jon? Come out, come out wherever you are!"

"Is that you, Tara?" Mrs Rogers called from upstairs.

"It's me, Maxine. Where's Jonathon?"

The woman appeared at the head of the stairs. "Jon? Why, isn't he with you?"

Tara was taken aback. "Well, no. We were exploring that old house and all of a sudden he just disappeared. We all thought he had come back here for lunch."

Little worry lines appeared between Mrs Roger's eyes. "Oh, I do hope he's not moping along the beach somewhere! He's been so…well…"

"Depressed," Tara finished gently. "I know. Honestly, Maxine, sometimes I think he ought to see a doctor."

Mrs Rogers' smile was twisted. "Your brother and I are trying very hard to trust the Lord with Jon's problem. We really believe it's more spiritual than it is physical, or even mental." She gazed at her young sister-in-law wistfully. "You will help us pray, won't you?"

Tara nodded solemnly. "I've already been praying. A lot. I know Jon loves Jesus. But, he's just so confused right now. And… well, he really holds it against my brother for moving him here and away from his friends."

Mrs Rogers sighed. "Yes, I know. We did think this move was right for the family, but with Jon's depression – and since he's just not snapping out of it – we're beginning to wonder." She came on down the stairs and headed for the kitchen. "But, Tara, you must be hungry, and I have a sandwich made for you."

Sitting at the kitchen table in front of a tuna fish sandwich and a glass of iced tea, Tara's eyes kept straying to the window. She did hope to see Jon coming along any second now.

Seeing her anxious look, Mrs Rogers suggested, "Maybe he walked into town for something to eat. I know he had money with him."

Tara was doubtful. "Maybe."

Mrs Rogers poured herself some iced tea and sat down across from Tara. Carefully squeezing a little lemon juice into her glass, she murmured softly, "Anyway, I'm sure he'll be home in time for supper, and I'm making his favourite food. Tacos." But now she, too, was watching out of the window. "Jon simply must understand that as parents, we are still in control of his life."

Tara did not answer, but she thought to herself that it would take a lot more than tacos to bring Jon out of his depression.

Mr Rogers had been in town nearly all day, and now he breezed into the room with a blank look. "Where's Jon?"

"You didn't see him in town or on the beach somewhere?" his wife inquired anxiously.

The man shrugged his wide shoulders and rubbed the stubble on his jaw. His smile turned into a frown. "No, why? Where is he?"

"We don't know."

"I know he likes to eat at that little place called The Pirate's Cove," Tara announced. "He likes their curly French fries and their crab burgers. Maybe he went there for lunch."

Mr Rogers looked both puzzled and annoyed. "I thought he was going with the rest of you kids today."

"He did," Tara replied carefully. "But he disappeared when we were exploring that old house."

Mr Rogers' face relaxed now and he shook his head. "Back there again, eh? You kids just can't stay away from that place, can you?"

Tara's dark eyes were eager and full of life now. "Oh Fred, you should see that house for yourself! It sure is big enough for an inn. We've been all over it and it's really awesome." Her pretty face suddenly darkened. "Of course, there's that awful organ playing funeral music and there's the baby crying and the footsteps when no one is there and – and all sorts of weird noises."

She almost told her brother about the secret room somewhere in the tower but decided against it. It was more fun to keep that a secret between the four youths for now.

Mr Rogers smiled and turned away. Over his shoulder he said, "When you see Jon, please tell him I need him to help me with some things."

Tara agreed. Finishing her sandwich and draining her glass of tea, she grabbed a couple of oatmeal cookies, left the house and trotted down the beach to find Woody and Renee.

"Tara!"

The shout came from far down the beach near the lighthouse as two figures came loping toward her. They met breathlessly but ready for more adventure. Woody was clutching a piece of wood in one hand and his knife in the other. Proudly he displayed the horse he was still working on.

"Oh Woody" Tara crooned, "it is truly beautiful! What a great job you've done with its head and mane. You can even pick out the separate hairs on its mane.

"He really is good," Renee beamed proudly. "In fact, some of his work is going up for sale at The Pirate's Cove."

"Woody, that's wonderful!"

A slow flush crept up Woody's tanned face. "But what I want to know is, where's Jon?"

Tara's eyes became troubled. "We don't know. We think he probably went into town, because he wasn't home when I got there, and no one seems to know where he is."

Woody's mouth turned down in disappointment. "Would he do that? Just take off without telling us where he was going?"

Tara bit her lip. "It doesn't sound like Jon, but," and she spread her arms helplessly, "where else could he be?"

Renee's freckled face was a study in thoughtfulness and confusion. "I know how much he hates it here, so I guess we shouldn't be surprised that he went off by himself." She turned and looked toward town. "I sure hope he's all right."

Woody checked his watch and, still holding the horse and the knife, tucked his thumbs in the waistband of his jeans. "It's two-thirty already, so I hope he doesn't stay away so long that he gets caught in the fog tonight." Looking dismal, he added ruefully, "I sort of thought Jon and I were becoming friends and that pretty soon he'd begin to like it here." He shook his head. "I guess I was wrong."

"But he does like you, Woody, I know he does," Tara soothed. "This doesn't have anything to do with you at all."

Still gloomy and disappointed, Woody mumbled, "Do you still want to go back inside the house?"

"It doesn't seem like as much fun without Jon," Renee sighed. "Why don't we give it up for today? We can go back there tomorrow when Jon is with us."

Woody went back to whittling his horse, looked around for a log to sit on and settled down for some serious work. "What do you want to do, then?"

"We could swim out to the rocks and scare the wits out of the man watching the house," Tara joked.

Woody was startled. "Don't tell me he's there again!"

"He was. I saw him when I went home for lunch. He pretended to be fishing, but I don't believe that at all."

Renee turned slowly and looked toward the rocks, glistening wet in the sunlight. "Why would anyone want to hang out there all the time?"

Woody had taken Tara seriously. "We can't swim out there now. The tide's all wrong and look how the water sucks back on itself. We'd be carried right out to sea." He stared toward the rocks, his knife and horse loose in his hands. "I don't see him now anyway."

"You can't ever see him from right in front of the old house, and he always ducks out of sight when he is seen" Tara hesitated. Then she added indignantly, "I know he's up to something, and I'd sure like to know what it is!"

The Stranger Approaches

Woody and the girls chose to ignore the mysterious old house the rest of that afternoon. Instead, they walked into town to search for Jon.

"It's hard for me to understand why Jon doesn't like it here," Woody mused, shuffling along beside the girls. "I've lived here so long – well, not here exactly, but on the east coast – that I really love it. The fishing, the smells, the ocean, the dopey porpoises and seals…"

Tara did not reply, she just kept trudging over the hard, wet sand thinking and praying. When they passed the strange house, they all gave it a suspicious look and went on. It looked so desolate and so forlorn sitting there next to the wooded area.

Finally voicing her thoughts, Tara said, "I still can't see how Jon ever got out of that place without our knowing it. At least one of us should have seen him leave."

Woody shrugged. "We were all pretty involved looking for a secret room."

Renee looked downright indignant. "I know he's your relative and all that, but I think he was awfully rude not to tell us he was leaving."

Behind them, walking along the road that led to his new home, Mr Rogers, too was on an errand. He did feel glad that the kids were going into town to look for Jonathon, and he fervently hoped that soon Jon would begin adjusting to living here.

Thrusting his hands into the pockets of his windbreaker, he stared at the ocean and sighed a shuddering sigh. "What if Jon doesn't adjust" he asked himself. "Then what? Moving here isn't worth losing my son over. Nothing is worth that." He lifted his dark eyes, so like Jon's, to the great white thunderheads crawling lazily across the sky. "What should I do, Lord? What is it that You want?"

Maybe he was crazy to be going to this old house, so full of mystery and secrets. It was probably a stupid dream to even think of purchasing it and turning it into an inn. Maybe he had rocks in his head to consider such an impossible venture.

The afternoon was about gone, and far out over the water a bank of fog was looming ominously. Neither he nor the kids had much time before it would be dark and fog would envelop the land.

With his hands still digging into his pockets, he stood in front of the massive structure and studied it carefully. "A grand old place in its day," he brooded aloud. "It could be again, I just know it." He sighed and rubbed his chin. "But it would require a lot of work. Oh well, Jon said the tower door is unlocked, so why don't I just take a quick look inside. It won't cost anything, and then maybe I can put this idea out of my mind."

Quickly he slipped into the chilly interior of the tower room, then on into the house. Almost at once he was aware of a baby crying in agony. Turning on his flashlight, he frowned, cocked his head, then he began to follow the sound. Common sense told him that it wasn't actually a baby crying – dead or alive.

For almost an hour he prowled through the house, often stopping to listen. Reaching the third floor, he at last discovered a tiny crack up near one window.

"Well, well," he droned, "I think I've found the crying baby."

Whipping out a handkerchief, he forced it into the crevice. Immediately the crying stopped and did not start again. Next he tracked down the bumping noise and found a loose shutter banging against the house.

He tapped walls, examined the floor and the ceiling, all with the practised eye of a building contractor.

"Old place was certainly built to last," he muttered softly. "It's sound as can be. Incredible after so many years." He nodded. "Yes, it would take a tremendous amount of work, but I know it's worth a great deal."

Finally, though, with daylight gone and the fog rolling in, he knew it was time to give up his investigation for today. One look out of a window told him that within an hour the land would be swallowed up in the grey mist that was steadily shuffling toward shore. He did hope the kids had returned from town and that they had found Jon.

He decided to try and leave by way of the front door and get home while he could still see. But a sound brought him up short. Quickly he turned off his light and ducked back into the shadowy recesses of a side room. There, he waited in silence.

Who on earth would be coming here at this hour? he asked himself. The kids wouldn't be coming back here this late, certainly not with the fog moving in.

Feeling foolish for hiding, still he did not move as the heavy oak door opened and a tall, broad-shouldered figure stalked inside the house. His light played around the area in front of him as if he were searching for something.

Slowly, cautiously, Mr Rogers stepped back a little farther, thankful that the floor was solid and he could move quietly. But he told himself that there were also bits of plaster and other rubble on the floor that could crunch beneath his shoes. For the truth was, he was starting to feel threatened by the presence of the stranger coming toward him.

The stranger was also walking very gingerly. His breath seemed loud in the stillness and he sounded like he was winded. Or perhaps he was only excited.

Mr Rogers peered around the corner and saw in the half-light that the man had a long, jagged scar on the left side of his face.

But why was he here? What was this all about?

Jon had given up the struggle to free himself. Instead, he wanted to cry terrified, outraged tears. But that would only make his nose stop up and then he wouldn't be able to breathe, not with the tape covering his mouth. Now he was left with only two wishes. No, three. He wished he could go to the bathroom, and he longed for a drink of water. His third and most important wish was that he was safe at home with his family.

Wait a minute. Home? The house on the beach? Surely he wasn't calling that place home!

"You do realize" the stranger asked casually, "that it was me who did you kids a big favour that night when those thugs were about to carry the girls away? I can tell you, it's not every night I'd be willing to put on some dusty old black dress to save someone."

Jon nodded eagerly and tried to smile, but the duct tape held his mouth shut. Anyway his eyes were not smiling, they were filled with terror. But surely a man who would save a couple of girls from being carried away into the night must have a soft spot in his heart somewhere.

Still, he had already told Jon that he was leaving tonight. It must almost be night by now. What then?

Suddenly the man put aside the carton of orange juice and looked at his watch. "Quarter-to-eight," he muttered.

He stood and then disappeared through the wall panel that Jon had thought himself so clever at discovering. But he was back, almost at once. Thrusting the gun into the waistband of his slacks and holding his knife in one hand, he jerked Jon to his feet. Bending, he neatly sliced through the tape binding Jon's ankles.

"I had almost decided to leave you here," the man explained shortly, "but I've changed my mind. You could be very good insurance in case something goes wrong." He motioned with his head towards the wall and snapped, "Let's go!"

Caught in the Crossfire

Jon was making muffled sounds behind the tape to ask where they were going. Oddly enough, the man understood him.

"You just be quiet and you'll find out soon enough."

Jon was prodded down the steps and into the main part of the house. Bulldog Face paused long enough to touch something that caused the wall panel to slide back into place. He told himself that it had been sheer good luck, his finding the secret room. What a great hiding place it had proved to be! It seemed like he had been hiding out there for ages, only going into town at night to steal food to bring back with him.

Now the man shoved Jon through the third floor to the steep stairs leading downward. With his hands behind his back and the flashlight giving very little light to see by, Jon stumbled down the steps, then tripped and fell three steps from the bottom.

The bulldog-face man jerked Jon to his feet again and led him through the second floor to the wide winding staircase that led to the first floor.

Cold, miserable and terrified, Jon wondered what horrible fate was in store for him. But the man had withdrawn his gun now, and with the cold barrel pushing into his back, he figured he didn't have any choice but to go along.

Something's different, he decided ruefully. The baby's not crying and the moaning and bumping noises have stopped.

Halfway down the grand stairway, they stopped and the man cocked his shaggy head to listen intently. Nothing! Nothing at all! Not even the usual creakings of an old house. It was as quiet as a graveyard.

"I'll just take this kid along with me until I'm sure I'm safe," Bulldog Face thought grimly. "Then I'll drop him off somewhere and forget him." He huffed with disgust. "Thank goodness for the fog. I hope it's too foggy out there for that blasted detective to be snooping around tonight."

He was thoroughly disgusted with the whole business. Hiding out just wasn't his thing. That nosy detective had traced him here, no doubt about that. He'd been watching this old house for days. It was kind of comical, too, he decided wryly. That detective had been all over the house and never had discovered the secret room. But then those kids had begun exploring the place and that had really cramped his style. He had known then that it was only a matter of time until he must deal with them. To think he had gone to so much trouble to save the girls that night, too!

Of course, the big problem now was making it through the fog and getting away, far away. He clenched his jaw. Well, it had to be done, and this kid was going to help him.

Jon thought he felt a rush of cold air swoop towards him and he frowned in confusion. However, Bulldog Face had not seemed to notice, he was too concerned with making his getaway. Ruthlessly he shoved Jon down the winding staircase.

The detective was sick and tired of spending his days out on the ridiculous pile of rocks. Even his binoculars were crusted with salt now and probably ruined. He wasn't exactly a young man, after all. He was tired and he just wanted this business to come to an end.

"But I know he's in that old house somewhere!" he grumbled dismally. "I can't let this thing go. I've always been like a bloodhound when it catches the scent of its prey." His sigh was vast. "Well, I've tracked him this far and I'm positive he hasn't yet made his getaway. But where is he?" Absently he fingered the scar on the left side of his face, a painful reminder of another criminal he had tracked down, one who had managed to knife him before the detective could duck.

"That night," he went on savagely, "I saw the light in the tower, I was so sure it was Luke Mortin stirring around." He huffed with frustration. "If I had rushed in there after him I'd have made a perfect fool of myself. Yeah. Good thing I looked in the window first and saw it was just one of the kids. That girl in the graveyard…ha! She didn't pay one bit of attention to my warning." He sighed again. "Well, those kids aren't in there tonight, I know that, so the light I saw has to be Luke. Thank goodness," he muttered fervently, "I'm finally going to get my man."

His flashlight was powerful and pierced the fog like an ice-pick. Coming to the big oak door, he pushed it open as quietly as possible, stepped inside and closed it again. In one hand was his light sweeping away the darkness, and in his other hand was a Colt .45. He wasn't going to fool around. Taking a deep breath, he snapped off his light and decided to wait for Luke to put in an appearance. When he did, Detective Lathan was ready for him.

Dead stillness surrounded him. No crying baby. No more moaning. No organ. No weird noises at all. Strange.

As time passed he began to fidget. He wanted a cigarette but knew the smell would give him away. He almost missed the old house's whisperings and moanings, for the silence seemed more ominous that the noises. Fumbling in a pocket, he brought forth a stick of gum, peeled away the paper with his teeth and chewed the gum fiercely. He sure hoped he wasn't going to have to wait very long in the cold, damp house.

A few feet away, Mr Rogers, too, was quiet and waiting. He dared not move even an inch lest some particle of plaster crunch underfoot. But he knew he wasn't alone; he simply had no idea who was occupying this old house with him. He just knew he felt threatened. Fearful.

On the stairs nearby, Luke Mortin had once more stopped to listen. His breathing was raspy and suspicious. His hold on Jon was strong, and Jon was smart enough to know that even if he tried to cry out, there was no one to hear his frantic call for help. Besides, such action could bring him a great deal of harm.

Bulldog Face lifted Jon firmly from the stairs and hauled him down a couple of steps. Again, for a long moment, he listened carefully. Satisfied that they were alone in the house, he shoved Jon on down the stairs and turned toward the front door.

"Can't be too careful," Luck told himself grimly. "You can't ever tell where that nosy detective will pop up. Snoopy old guy, he ought to retire. Well, I have a hostage, and as long as the kid is in front of me, he wouldn't dare try and stop me."

Jon felt sick to his stomach. He had read about hostage situations and how dangerous they could be. "Jesus," he cried in desperation, "I know I don't deserve Your help, but I sure hope You won't let this guy kill me!"

Bulldog Face pushed Jon toward the hall leading to the door, when a brilliant light suddenly shone into their faces. Jon had no idea who was behind that light, but if he could have broken free he would have rushed to the person's side and clung to them.

"It's all over, Mortin," said the detective firmly. "Let the boy go."

Startled, Luke stumbled back a step, taking Jon with him. "Not on your life!" he snarled. "Get out of my way or the kid is dead."

Afterwards, trying to piece it all together, it seemed that a number of things happened all at the same time. Luke's arm was tight about Jon as he forced the boy ahead of him. The detective went into a firing position but was afraid to get off a shot lest he hit Jon by mistake. Then swiftly a shadowy figure dived from out of nowhere and flung himself at Jon, knocking him harmlessly to the floor. Instantly shots began ringing out and one of the men went down. It was confusion after that as the two men left standing tried to sort it all out.

More shots were fired. There was a loud, angry curse and Bulldog Face joined the man on the floor.

Utterly confused, Jon got to his feet and backed against the wall, trembling. Dimly he heard the detective mumbling to himself, for he was still stunned by the appearance of another man nearby who had moved to protect the boy.

It was only when the detective shone his light on the face of the first man to go down that Jon realized with horror who it was.

The tape holding his wrist had torn when Jon was knocked to the floor, and now, savagely, he wrenched free. In one swift motion he tore away the tape from his mouth. With an animal-like scream of rage and disbelief, he cried, "NOOOOOOO! Dad, no! Oh please, God, not my dad!"

Home

Guilt and fear washed through Jon like water through a broken dam as he stared in horror at his father lying in a pool of blood. All the bitterness and resentment were gone in an instant. He had visions of himself refusing to speak to his father. Ignoring him. Trying to hurt him for this move to the east coast.

Who did he think he was anyway? Fred Rogers was still the father and he, Jonathon, was a rotten kid who thought he knew everything.

Unaware of Detective Lathan standing there in shock with his gun hanging limply at his side, Jon flung himself at his dad's bleeding form and sobbed.

He wasn't even aware of Bulldog Face doubled up, in agony a few feet away.

Mr Rogers had taken one bullet in his thigh and another in his left shoulder. Having been caught in the crossfire, he had caught slugs from both the detective's gun and Luke Mortin's. Now, feebly, he reached for Jon with his right arm.

Babbling hysterically, Jon pleaded, "Dad, don't die, please don't die! Oh God, please don't let my dad die!"

The detective snatched him to his feet. "Now you listen to me, son! We've got two men here who are bleeding to death. You hear?" When Jon sniffed and wiped away tears with the back of his hands, the man went on. "I've got to have you help, do you understand?"

Jon's vision was blurred by his tears. The detective's words went right over him. "Dad, I'm so sorry, I'm so sorry! Please, can you forgive me for the way I've acted?"

A limp smile touched Mr Rogers' face. "Of course I for...give..." But he was fading into unconsciousness and could not finish the sentence.

Dragging sick eyes back to Detective Lathan, Jon muttered, "What do you want me to do?"

The detective was coming to life himself. He had never in all his years as a detective run into a situation like this. He whipped out his cell phone and dialled a number. To Jon he said crisply, "Take these handcuffs and get them on Mortin. Now!" he yelled when Jon hesitated. Turning his attention to the phone he called for two ambulances. Surely, living on the east coast, they would have lights to penetrate that thick soup out there.

The next afternoon found Jon trudging along the beach to where Woody sat whittling. Sensing Jon approach, he smiled and held up the horse he was still working on.

"What do you think?"

Jon sat down just beyond the long string of seaweed lining the beach. "It looks great, Woody. You're really good."

"It's for Tara," Woody said shyly. "Do you think she'll like it?"

"Are you kidding? She'll be crazy about it."

For a moment they sat in companionable silence, and then Woody ventured hesitantly, "You don't look too happy."

Jon grunted.

Woody laid the knife in his lap. "Do you want to talk about it?"

"My dad's going to make it okay." Jon's voice was barely above a whisper.

Woody sensed that it was important to get his friend talking. "Can you tell me everything that happened? The last thing we knew, you had disappeared and we thought you'd gone into town for something." He inspected the horse again, smoothed a tiny trouble spot with a piece of fine sandpaper, and then he ran his thumb over it. "I'm still pretty much in the dark about a lot of things."

Jon blew out his breath, still wearing a mask of gloom. "I found the secret room and decided to take a quick look before telling the rest of you." He waved a hand through the air. "Big mistake. Old Luke – I started calling him Bulldog Face to myself, because he looked like a bulldog – slapped his hand over my mouth, dragged me back in the room and tied me up with duct tape."

Woody had stopped fingering the wooden horse and sat staring at Jon incredulously.

"Luke was wanted for two murders in Boston, I found out later, and he was hiding out in that old house. He'd found the hidden room by accident, so he stayed there and went into town sometimes at night for food."

Woody's grey eyes were envious. He did wish he could have been in on the excitement! "And the detective? I know he was the guy hanging out on the rocks watching the house."

"Sure. Detective Lathan had tracked Luke this far and was positive he was hiding in the house but could never find him." Jon shrugged. "So he hung out on those rocks pretending to fish. Every time he saw a light in the house he was sure he was going to catch him. Except one time it was me, and another time, it was the two of us. Then last night he was sure no one was in the house – none of us, that is – and when he saw Dad's light he thought he had his man."

"He sneaked inside the house and waited, and when Luke forced me down the stairs with him, Detective Lathan shone his light in our eyes. He was shocked to see me in front of Luke, and then my dad leaped out of the shadows…" Jon blew out his breath grimly. "That's when Dad got caught in the crossfire."

Woody gave a silent whistle. "All the time the man with the scar was the detective."

"Right." Jon idly chewed the side of his thumb. "All the spooky noises we heard? Dad tracked down some of them, and they were just caused by ordinary things like a loose shutter and the wind whistling through crevices. Of course Luke made some of the sounds to try and scare us away."

"Sure takes the adventure out of it," Woody said whimsically.

Jon's laugh was limp. "Sort of."

Woody murmured softly, "I have a question."

"Okay."

"Since things are all right between you and your dad again, and since he's going to get well…why are you still so gloomy?"

Jon's sigh was ragged. "I guess," he faltered, "I'm having a real hard time forgiving myself for the way I've treated my dad." He waved a hand through the air. "I know he's forgiven me, and I know God's forgiven me, but my attitude has been so rotten – and when I saw my dad willing to die for me anyway…"

Woody nodded, frowning. "But isn't that what Jesus did for you? Died for you when you didn't deserve it?"

The question startled Jon. "You talk like I used to talk."

"I've been doing a lot of thinking," Woody confessed slowly.

"Wow, and I've been such an awful witness to you, Woody. I'm truly sorry for that."

Woody bit his lip, then asked hesitantly, "Are you going to be all right here? You do have a couple of new friends, you know."

Jon's smile was slow and wistful. "I'll be okay, and I'm thankful for new friends. But, see, I learned something through all this: I found out that home is where your mum and dad are."

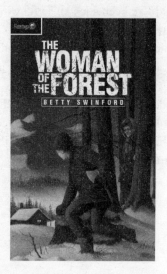

The Cry of the Wild

Scott was seized with horror. He felt like he was caught up in a whirlwind and his world was falling apart around him. Behind him, a smug-faced Ricky was smiling slyly...

ISBN 1 85792 853 9

Rocky Mountain Adventures

Join in the Rocky Mountain Adventure – set out on the trail that will teach you about this wonderful mountain range and the amazing God who created it.

ISBN 1 85792 962 4